THE MYSTERY OF THE MAGIC MIRROR

THE MYSTERY OF THE MAGIC MIRROR

SHUBIRA PRASAD

LET KNOWLEDGE SPREAD

Published by
Renu Kaul Verma
Vitasta Publishing Pvt Ltd
4348/4C, Ansari Road, Daryaganj
New Delhi - 110 002
info@vitastapublishing.com

वत्स an imprint of Vitasta Publishing

ISBN: 978-81-19670-64-2

First Edition 2024
MRP ₹250

Edited by Vichtra Goel
Cover Design by Somesh Kumar Mishra
Typeset by Rohit Gotam
Printed at Chaman Enterprises, New Delhi

To

My father, Late Shri Anant Swarup,
from whom I inherited my profound love for
reading and writing.

Contents

Living With The Dead

As was his habit the ghost went around the whole house ensuring everything was in place and as normal as yesterday. It had been his habit for a few years now, that is, from the time he had died. It was his house earlier and even now. He liked the peace and tranquillity of his home that had been undisturbed till now. But lately, he had been getting very disturbed.

The worst part was that when things were carelessly thrown around, he could not do anything about them. The ghost did not have the energy and strength to pick up things and put them in their proper places. For, you see, after his death, he had become like the wind, maybe a bit thicker, and that was all he was. He could think, thank goodness for that, but he could not do anything else. He would roam about the house, run or float around fast, and hide in one of the rooms upstairs when this odious family woke up in the morning.

Shailendra opened his eyes to the sound of silence. He closed his eyes again, trying to go back to sleep, but tossed and turned instead as sleep eluded him. He was ten years old, and his sister Opal was seven. Opai was such a unique name; his Bua had chosen it. Whereas his name, Shailendra, was chosen by his parents. He did not mind his name as much as he disliked the distortions that his friends and relatives did. They called him Shailu, Shally, or Inder, as his dadi called him lovingly. But it was in school that his classmates distorted his name. They called him 'Cylinder'. So much so that sometimes he even responded to it. But it was all done in fun and love, and he did not really dislike all the epithets. It just made him sometimes feel that he was more than one person.

Shailendra was a fun-loving boy, a little too fun-loving at times, but he was not wicked. He liked to make fun of things and people but did not want to hurt them or make them angry. He was a strong boy, a little too tall for his age. He was always in jeans and a T-shirt and liked to walk with his hands in his front pockets. As a result, it looked as if his jeans would fall any minute, but it never happened. He had a square face with a mop of thick hair. Some hair covered his right eye, which he flipped back unconsciously while thinking seriously. He had twinkling eyes, ready to laugh at everything and everybody. His eyes crinkled at the corners even when he did not laugh. It looked as if he was always looking for a reason to smile. His eyes were pure mischief, but he had a heart of gold.

Like any other boy his age, he was very fond of using the mobile phone, not for chatting with his friends but because of all the apps a mobile phone provides nowadays. His parents sometimes allowed him to use his father's spare mobile phone. It was the best reward he could think of. There was so much to do on a mobile—he played games, watched YouTube, and did many other things. For this reason, his parents did not give him the phone too often. They wanted him to go and play outside, which had temporarily stopped because of Covid-19, and secondly, he had not made any friends in their new locality.

Opal was his sweet sister. Shailendra loved her to bits and could do anything for her. He loved even her name. His parents had no problem naming her. His father had bought an opal necklace for his mother. She loved it so much that she decided to call her daughter Opal, whenever she had her. And she was just like an opal—sweet and pink and white. Her hair was like waves of the earth, curled and soft, bouncing when she moved. It seemed as if Opal never spoke; she sang, her voice tinkling like raindrops in a glass. When she spoke, everybody listened to her, mesmerised by her sweet voice. When she smiled, her eyes lit up, and so did everything around. Sometimes, the ghost felt she was the most beautiful girl on earth.

It never seemed that she was walking, she was, as if, floating. Their mother dressed Opal in soft and silky clothes that floated with her. But her resemblance to a delicate fairy-like girl was limited till here. For Opal was quite a wicked yet practical girl. Though she was wicked, she was not evil; when somebody was wicked to her, she would be equally wicked and sometimes even more.

Although Opal was three years younger than her elder brother Shailendra, she was the one to lead them into an adventure and even get out of it. One of the reasons that they managed to come out of any situation without any harm was because the adults found it easier to believe Opal. Even at this early age, Opal's parents knew that Opal was unique. She was intelligent, funny, pretty, sporting, and warm.

The brother and sister shared a special, unbreakable bond. Though Shailendra had this protective, elder brother attitude towards her, in reality, Opal protected him more.

Sometimes, while playing in the garden, Shailendra would lie in the grass pretending to be asleep. The ghost had watched this over and over again. When his little sister Opal came to wake him up, he would not wake up but instead play dead. He would even stop breathing and wait for her to come closer. Then he would jump up like a tightly rolled spring and roar louder than a lion, his arms widely flying everywhere. He would cover his face with his hair, trying to look fierce and savage. Opal would scream with delight and try to look scared and horrified. Instead, she would shriek with delight and ask her brother to do it again. She would fall on the grass, clap her hands, and jump up and down, giggling the whole time. Then, he would promptly fall again as if he was shot and the game would begin again.

So it was because of Covid that they had to come and live in this house. It was very far off from the beautiful home where they lived earlier. Their father had been given notice from his comfortably paying job, and now he was working in another company for a much lower salary. Their father had told them they would return to the city as soon as he got a better job. They had shifted to this house on the city outskirts as one of their relatives had given it to them at a very nominal price.

Even though this house was big and had a fair number of rooms, it was so drab and old that it smelt of old rotting wood and clothes. There were not many houses nearby. Initially, their mother, Neelam, was dismayed when she saw the house. It was a big, rambling, two-storied house, but very dark and grey!

But not for long. Opal had got her sunny disposition from her mother only. Neelam took only one day to go over the house and then sat with her husband and children to decide how to renovate the home and make it cheerful. Within a week, the house had started looking bright and happy. Their father Hemant hired a few labourers to clean up the surroundings, like hacking the weeds and trimming the trees, and mowing the overgrown grass in the lawn. Neelam cleaned the cobwebs in the home, and

Hemant got painters to clean and whitewash the walls and paint the doors and windows. Neelam was a painter; she hung her many beautiful paintings on the walls. That, along with bright curtains, brought quite a lot of cheer to the house. It had begun looking inviting even if a stranger walked past it.

Later they learnt that nobody had lived in this house for a very long time, because many people from one family had died here without any reason. Of course, their parents did not tell this to them, but Opal had her sources. It was she who informed Shailendra about the ghost.

'Nonsense,' said Shailendra, 'There is no such thing as ghosts. When the wind blows through the wet trees, it makes a sound. People think that it is a ghost. Sometimes, a cat jumps quietly and runs away, but in its jumping, some utensils or other things fall, making a sound. People don't see the cat, so they think it is a ghost,' he said confidently.

'Bhaiya,' Opal said equally confidently, 'You don't know anything. The house is full of ghosts.'

Experience had taught Shailendra that though Opal always spoke her mouth off and made up grand stories at the drop of a hat, there would still be a grain of truth in whatever she proclaimed. Shailendra paused. If Opal was so confidently saying that there were ghosts, then there must be at least one ghost or two.

'Hmm,' but he was not going to give in so quickly, 'How can you say so?' he countered, 'Have you seen any ghosts?'

'Of course, bhaiya, just the other day, I saw a ghost. It was sitting in the front room, trying to read a newspaper.

But the newspaper kept slipping out of his hands because he could not hold it. As you know, ghosts are made of wind and minute mist particles. They don't have any strength. They have to drink blood to have strength and move about.'

Without realising it, Shailendra got caught in Opal's trap. He began thinking on her lines.

'What was this ghost doing when you saw him?'

Opal became more comfortable now as she had her brother's full attention.

'Bhaiya, he was sitting on the sofa in the corner. He picked up the newspaper or tried to pick it up, but it was too heavy for him. After a lot of struggles, he managed to pick it up and tried to open it. It was while he was occupied with it that I went there. I was horrified.'

'What did he look like?' Shailendra was now all agog with curiosity. He was a bit fearful as well. Imagine! A ghost in his house. Wait till he told his friends. But Opal could read her brother's thoughts.

'No, bhaiya, we will keep this an absolute secret. We won't tell anybody. If Ma and Papa get to know about it, they may think of changing this house and then all the fun will be gone. We came to this house because it was cheap. Ma and Papa won't be able to afford another house till Papa pays off all his debts and finds a better-paying job.'

'That's right,' Shailendra agreed, 'We won't tell anybody. What did he look like, Opal, and what did he do when he saw you?'

Seeing that she had finally got her brother's attention, Opal acted a bit pricey now. Not too much, though. Bhaiya would still not believe her and go away. She had to make her story more interesting. Her voice dropped to a whisper, '*Aise toh* bhaiya, he wasn't a big-sized ghost. He looked just like a slim, old man, and was shimmering and swaying. Just as he tried to sit, a gush of wind came from the window. His upper body looked like flying with the wind, but he controlled himself and sat on the sofa.'

Opal kept quiet for a few minutes, then realised that if she wanted Shailendra on her side, then she would have to tell him everything, even if he made fun of her.

'Bhaiya, remember the magnifying glass which mummy sometimes uses?'

'Yes, what about it?'

'Bhaiya, that is how I saw this ghost. I was playing with the magnifying glass, just looking here and there through it, when suddenly I saw this transparent shadow. When I removed the glass, he had disappeared. I couldn't find him after that, because mummy asked for the magnifying glass back as she wanted to read the small print on some medicine. I didn't ask for the glass again because I saw the ghost again trying to sit on the sofa.'

Shailendra was impressed by the information. He tried not to believe her but got caught in her web of stories again.

'Okay, that means he does not have strength at all,' Shailendra thought loudly.

'Bhaiya,' Opal whispered again, 'You think he'll become stronger by drinking human blood?'

Shailendra was stunned. Oh yes! Isn't this what ghosts were famous for–scaring people and drinking their blood?

Opal was in her element now, but Shailendra was not to be trapped so easily. He did become nervous for a few minutes, but he also knew that his sister could spin long yarns and usually was even successful in convincing people. Sometimes, when their parents were indulgent, they marvelled at her storytelling art. Opal spoke of her fantasies as if she believed them completely. Probably, that was the reason her stories were so convincing. Shailendra was a frequent victim of this. He knew now that he had to see proof of these before believing. What was there not to believe? A bored ten-year-old boy with very few friends whom he could not meet frequently because they had just changed their house. A ghost in their house! Well, there was nothing to do except to catch him. But wait! What if there was more than one ghost? The hair on his arms rose. How thrilling! Shailendra just hoped that Opal was right, or else things would become dull and boring again. So, things depended on Opal now.

'You will have to show me next time you see him,' he said imperatively, pulling rank on her. Under normal circumstances, Opal just pooh-poohed his seniority, but today, she had to prove her point. If they had to catch the ghost, she needed to convince bhaiya that she had, indeed, seen a ghost. Opal accepted everything in her life; she was always happy. She found the world interesting, where everybody loved and liked each other. But then, most of the time, she was in her world, thinking and making up stories as she grew up.

'I think there is more than one ghost, bhaiya,' she declared, her lips and eyes round with awe and excitement. 'I have seen it twice, bhaiya, both times on the living room sofa, trying to read the newspaper unsuccessfully.'

'What happened after that? Did he manage to read the paper?'

'I don't think so. He was so busy trying to hold himself against the wind. He was just getting blown away, at times his upper body and sometimes his lower body. I don't think he has any strength. Ultimately he got up in disgust and just walked out through that door.'

'Oh! Which door?' Shailendra was caught up in Opal's story again.

'That door, bhaiya,' she pointed at the door which led to the veranda and out.

'Did you follow him?' Shailendra narrowed his eyes in suspicion and anticipation.

'No, bhaiya, I was scared; he had not noticed me. What if he did? I wanted to call you, bhaiya, but he had disappeared by then. I think we will wait for him after breakfast and see if he comes to read the newspaper.'

'What does he look like?' Shailendra was engrossed, 'Does he look like a demon or like us?'

'No, bhaiya, he doesn't look like a demon at all, nor does he look like us. He looked more like a flowy thing as if someone had covered a bamboo pole with a large, thin sheet. I could even see through the sheet. There was nothing inside the sheet. But he looked like a tall thin man when he sat on the sofa. The window beside the

sofa was open; a small gust of wind blew him away.'

Shailendra nodded excitedly. They had dinner and went to bed, though Shailendra could hardly sleep now. But there was still the doubt whether Opal spoke the truth or was recounting one of her stories.

The ghost was sitting outside in the so-called garden. There was a slight drizzle, and a gentle wind was blowing. First, he did not have any energy, and secondly, whatever little energy he had was spent in getting the parts of his body back. He was just a flowy shadow, somehow confined to this house. He had been quite happy and content to live the rest of his ghost life here in this house. It was his house. He used to live here when he was alive. So he would continue to live here now that he was dead and a ghost. Why should I leave my house and live in some other place? He asked nobody in general but just spoke to himself.

Until a month ago, he could shimmer around anywhere in the house, upstairs or downstairs, lie down anywhere, and generally do nothing. Maybe he would have done something if he only knew what ghosts were supposed to do. He knew that to survive, he had to eat something. He was a ghost, so he could not have regular human food. He had heard that ghosts drank blood to become strong. It was a misnomer that ghosts drank only human blood, in fact, any blood would do as long as it was blood. But the very thought of drinking blood was abhorrent to him. As a result, he was weak and always tottering around, sometimes just vanishing because of a lack of ghostly food, that is blood. He did not miss food too much. He was a picky eater even when he was alive. He did not like to eat at all. When he was alive, his mother, wife, and daughter would ensure that something went inside his stomach. But when he died and became a ghost, there was no one to feed him forcefully. He did not know how and what to eat.

Sometimes, when his stomach grumbled too much, he would go to the shrubbery jungle behind his house and try to eat the worms or caterpillars. He always gagged on them. Once, he caught an almost dead bird. Since it was dying, he drank its blood but vomited immediately. But the little trace of the blood in his body gave him enough strength for the next two days.

Overall Ghosty was quite happy and comfortable in this house. It was his house, where he had spent most of his childhood and youth. Later, he had to shift to another city because of his job. After his retirement, he returned and then died mysteriously. Now, he was all alone in this house. Sometimes, he thought about all the people in his life. He was always uncomfortable in their company. He did not miss anybody. Sometimes, he missed his wife and daughter, but that was only at times. He was free now of all the worldly disturbances.

But all his ghostly freedom and comfort was lost

when this family came to live here. The parents were not troublesome; he could still tolerate them. But the children were so noisy and mischievous that they gave Ghosty a perpetual headache. He had to run around, trying to escape their wild and unruly actions. Ghosty could easily tolerate the boy Cylinder. Although he always thought: How can anybody be called a Cylinder? Was he a gas cylinder or a drum of some kind? Anyway, the living could call anyone anything.

It was the girl Opal who always scared the life out of him. Not that he had any life, but he still had his dignity and wanted to stay peacefully. It was just the other day when he was trying to sit on the sofa to read the newspaper, which he had not read for decades, the audacious girl saw him getting blown here and there by the wind. It was so embarrassing. Forget about holding the newspaper, he could not even hold himself. There was no dignity now that these people had taken over the house–his house. How dare they come and settle here! But he could not do anything. He could not speak, at least not the way he used to when he was alive. Now, the only sound which came out of his mouth was a kind of whooshing, which people brushed off as a cold gust of wind. He never wanted to go anywhere near the humans; it just happened. The times when he got something nutritious to eat, his eyes glowed, not for long, just for half an hour or so.

But the main point was that he was disturbed by the living people here. First of all, the pesky children played and fought and got boisterous. Then there was the couple who was always busy. In the process, they made noises that Ghosty abhorred. He had forgotten what life was like when he was living. Now that he was living like a ghost and liking it, these living people were disturbing him. They raked up his long-lost memories, some of which were the good ones. For instance, one thing over which he had slight control was his nose. He could make out the different kinds of smells. He liked the sweet scent of flowers; he disliked the smell of rotting wood and fungus. It was his nose which was rebelling against the presence of these living people. But things gradually began to change.

The lady of the house, Shailendra's, and Opal's mother, was an excellent cook. Consequently, the kitchen and the dining room became Xoxo's (Ghosty's) favourite places to hang around. Later somehow, the name Xoxo stuck to him when Opal started calling him Xoxo because there was a 'Xuxu' sound whenever she caught him running. She did not like Xuxu, so she named him Xoxo instead. So here was Opal's mother, Neelam, who cooked with so much love and care that everybody looked forward to food and relished their meals. Many a time, their father would help their mother in the kitchen. To begin with, he tasted everything Neelam made, not once but twice, and gave suggestions like 'I think a little more salt is required', 'no, don't add sugar, the kheer is naturally sweet now', or 'Ohh! Nobody can make stuffed chicken like you, even if you give them the recipe.' Saying so, he would kiss his wife's hands while she smiled and glowed in his praise.

Hearing so much of a commotion in the kitchen, one day, Xoxo decided to enter the kitchen. To be honest, Xoxo came to the kitchen because of the flavourful aromas. It was the only thing that he had as a ghost. Probably, God had heightened this propensity in him as he did not drink blood or kill anybody. Gradually, Xoxo found himself frequenting the kitchen more often.

Initially, he was just satisfied by inhaling the exquisite warm aromas, later he noticed that he equally liked to watch them eating and drinking. Somehow, he felt his hunger lessening when he breathed in the redolent aromas of the food and watched them eat and drink with full gusto. He watched in fascination as they guzzled, gulped, slurped, or washed down the chicken biryani with either a soft drink or beer their father had. They were four people; their father would sit at the head of the table, while their mother would sit on his left and serve all of them. Her seat was near the kitchen since it was convenient to go 'to and fro' from the kitchen. Shailendra and Opal generally sat on chairs on the side. That left the chair on the other head free. Xoxo made it a point to sit there and watch the proceedings. After observing them for a few days, he began the make-believe game of directing them. He would look at Shailendra, asking him to eat the chicken with the chapati and a bite of the freshly made salad. He liked to hear the crunch when Shailendra chewed on the salad. He would then direct their father, Hemant to eat slowly, so that he could enjoy the food more. Sometimes, he would order their mother, Neelam, to bring fresh chapatis or parathas.

But Xoxo gave a wide berth as far as Opal was concerned. He feared that any interaction with Opal would expose him. Opal had seen him at times. If she noticed him at their dining table, she would surely raise a ruckus, ending his play-acting. He ordered the other three people to do his bidding because he had closely observed their behaviour and could pre-empt it without anybody being any wiser. Sometimes, when he spoke harshly to 'Cylinder' or admonished Neelam when she was a little late in bringing the chapatis, he would get blown away by his own words or fall in a heap on the ground. He would quickly scramble back on his chair, huffing and puffing the whole time. By the time he reassembled himself, they would have finished and gone. This left him disappointed!

After Opal's revelations, Shailendra woke up early. He was too excited. Maybe they would see the ghost this morning. He impatiently waited for Opal to wake up. He dared not wake her up, as he had learnt from experience. Opal was always in a bad mood after waking up in the mornings, so much so that even her parents did not wake her on the holidays. Shailendra tip-toed everywhere for fear of waking up Opal and maybe scaring off the ghost.

Finally, Opal woke up after what seemed like ages to Shailendra. It was 7.30 am. Surprisingly, Opal was in a good mood. Shailendra was having his breakfast. The ghost was also sitting there, inhaling the aroma of the food. They could not see him. Opal, too, sat on one of the chairs, having her milk. She looked at the milk for some time, then remembered about yesterday. Oh, yes, today bhaiya was going to be with her when the ghost came. Her eyes brightened as she looked at Shailendra. He was also looking at her. They both smiled at each other conspiratorially.

After finishing their breakfast, they went and sat opposite the sofa where the ghost sat. Suddenly, Opal put her finger on her lips, signalling him to be quiet. Shailendra became very excited. Opal shushed him again. He settled down in the chair, fully alert. They waited for fifteen minutes, but nothing happened. Shailendra was very disappointed, 'I am going now; there is no ghost here.' He got up from the chair, but Opal pulled him back. He looked at her. She was looking straight at the sofa. Shailendra, too, sat down quietly and stared at the sofa. He could not see anything. But wait! He saw a rustle of the newspaper kept on the bamboo basket beside the sofa.

Every morning, the day's newspaper would be kept in the basket for anyone to read whenever they wanted to. He saw a movement as if somebody was trying to pick it up. The ghost! He looked intently, his body quivering, ready to jump. Jump at what, where? He didn't know. He had forgotten about Opal's presence, too. Now, he could see a shadow-like figure bending over the newspaper basket. Shailendra jumped up in his excitement. That was the end of everything. The shadow sat up straight for a

moment, then glided towards the veranda door and vanished.

'Bhaiya! What have you done? You've scared it away. Now I don't know when it will return,' Opal was genuinely upset; her eyes had become moist.

'I'm sorry, Opal,' Shailendra stammered, 'I didn't mean to frighten it. I was so surprised that I got up voluntarily. I won't do it again, I promise.'

But Opal was not convinced, 'I don't know whether it'll come tomorrow or not,' she went out, leaving Shailendra red-faced.

***

Now You See Me, Now You Don't

The ghost did not come the next day or the next. It did not come at all. After the third day, both the brother and sister were sitting in the veranda, thinking about the ghost. They were sipping on the orange juice their mother had freshly squeezed for the whole family. The ghost loved the smell of fresh oranges, too. So whenever Neelam took out the oranges from the fruit basket, he followed her to the kitchen, giving his expert suggestion, 'You know, Neelam, you must add some roasted cumin seeds and a pinch of black salt to make it tastier.' Neelam, of course, didn't see or hear anything, but she was surprised when she found herself adding black salt to the juice. She heaved a sigh of relief when the children liked it.

'Bhaiya, I think the ghost has changed his place. We have to find where he roams in the house now.'

'Opal, this is such a huge house. There are so many rooms upstairs and downstairs. Mummy gets the extra rooms cleaned, and then she bolts them. What if he is in those rooms?'

They sat thinking of their problem. It was their summer holidays. They had nothing much to do except some projects which their teachers had given them as homework. As they had completed half of their projects, there was no nagging from their mother to complete the rest. Neelam knew that they would finish them. But what surprised Neelam was the camaraderie between brother and sister. Usually, they would argue and squabble over small matters. But now, during these holidays, they seemed to have become friends. Neelam glanced at them from the kitchen window and crossed her fingers. It was so peaceful with the children not fighting. It gave her more time to work on hobbies like gardening and painting. She would have been horrified had she known what Shailendra and Opal were planning about. Neelam could not hear them, but she could make out that, as usual, Opal was leading the conversation.

'Bhaiya, we have to catch him; I have an idea. We'll tie a thin thread on both sides of all the doors so that he trips on them and falls. That way, we will see him and maybe catch him too.'

'Good idea, Opal,' Shailendra praised her, 'But what

if he trips at night when we are sleeping? He seems very light, so there may not be any sound when he falls.'

'Yes,' Opal said wistfully, then brightened up, 'What we'll do is take our chances. If we catch him, good. In the meantime, we will think of better ideas.'

Shailendra brightened up. He wanted to see the ghost. His one glimpse of the ghost made him want more. Off they went and got a grey-coloured reel from their mother's sewing basket and started from the top. They tied a single strand of thread horizontally to both sides of a door. They tied it about six inches above the ground so that the ghost gets entangled. They worked furtively so that their parents did not see them. It took them quite a lot of time to do all the doors, and they were still unsure whether Xoxo the ghost would fall for the trap. They were tired after their evening's work, so off to sleep they went.

The next day, Opal jumped up from her bed. She was very excited. She ran to Shailendra's room (they had separate bedrooms because this house was too big and had many rooms). She pulled back Shailendra's quilt, 'Wake up, bhaiya, we have to check the threads!'

For a minute, Shailendra just sat on the bed, and then last night's memory hit him like a hammer. He bounced off his bed, 'Let's go,' he ordered Opal and off they went. The thread on the door of their parents' room was broken. But that could be because mummy and papa may have gone without suspecting anything, and the thread broke without them noticing it. So, this room didn't count. Quickly, they went to the other rooms. Sure enough, there were two rooms upstairs which had broken threads. They looked triumphantly at each other. So, the ghost must have tripped on these threads, breaking all of them. It proved their theory that the ghost was indeed living in their house.

Now their next job or adventure would be to catch the ghost red-handed. Hurriedly, they bathed, made beds, ate breakfast, and sat in the living room with their juices. If their mother was surprised by their good behaviour, she did not comment as she was too relieved by the peace in the house.

In such matters, Opal was the one with ideas. But now, even she could not think of the next step. For one thing, it was not a destructive ghost. It must be just trying to roam around in the house, trying to read the newspaper. Newspaper! Yes! That was it! That was where they had first seen the ghost.

'I have an idea, Oppie,' When he was excited, Shailendra would call her Oppie.

'What, bhaiya, tell me fast.'

'We'll put paint on the tops of the newspapers after Papa and Mummy have read them. So when Xoxo picks up the newspaper from the basket, his hands will be smeared from the paint. This paint will not go away in a hurry, and this way, we will be able to catch him.'

Opal's eyes grew big with delight, 'Oh, bhaiya, that's an amazing idea. But where will we get the paint from?'

'Not to worry, Oppie. Remember when we were shifting to this house, Papa and Mummy got the whitewashing and painting done? Some of the paint is still lying in the garage. We can take some of it. We don't require much, just about half a cup of paint.'

'What is it I hear, Shailendra? What paint?' asked Neelam.

Both the children jumped up guiltily, 'Oh, Mummy, our holidays have just begun, and we have finished most of our projects. You do so much work in the garden. We thought we'd paint the lower portion of a few trees with the leftover paint. They will look pretty.'

'Oh!' Neelam looked at them suspiciously. Shailendra and Opal looked back at their mother innocently. It was such a simple and flawless excuse that she agreed and went back to continue her painting. The children gave a thumbs up to each other but giggled nervously. If only their mother suspected the actual use of the paint, she would have been horrified. Plus, she would have barred them from entering the garage, used as a part-time store. There would have been a real drama if their mother knew about the ghost.

So, off they went to the garage, took some white and red paint, and went to a nearby tree where their mother could see them. They then cleaned the tree, dried it with a cloth, and painted about three feet of its trunk with white paint. Their mother saw them with the corner of her eye. The paint looked scratchy on the tree trunk, but she said nothing. It was good that they had left small patches here and there. This gave the tree enough space to breathe. Neelam absentmindedly thought of these things while she painted. Shailendra

and Opal feverishly painted the trunk of one tree, then another. Finally, their mother packed up her painting stuff and went inside. It was getting dark. Mummy must have packed her things because the sunlight was fading. The children heaved a sigh of relief. It was late evening. Their father would soon return, and their parents would have tea on the veranda. After that, their mother would go to the kitchen to prepare dinner. That meant that the children were free till dinner.

Furtively, they went inside the living room where the newspapers were kept. Opal had half a cup of red paint in her hand. Quickly, they went to the newspaper basket and smeared the red paint over the newspapers kept on top. They hid their work with a clean newspaper; they would remove it at night. They had to be careful, or their parents would find out.

He had been so happy here in this house. It was his house when he was alive and is still his house after his death. The problem was that, earlier, he could verbally tell people they were not welcome and that they should not visit him. He had been quite happy even after his death. Except for a couple of weeks after his death when he had to adjust to his new life, nothing much had changed. He was in the same house with no people around.

These children, the pests, were making Xoxo miserable. The other day, he fell thrice because these wicked children had tied threads on the doors, and he tripped on them. He wasn't hurt, but his self-respect and ego got bruised. How he longed for a quiet house without any noise, without anybody disturbing him in his nocturnal walks whenever he wanted. Now, let alone peaceful walks, he could not wander from one room to another without tripping over something. These pests had started tying threads for him to trip over. Everything had become topsy-turvy ever since they had come here.

Xoxo decided he would not wander or float from one room to another but stay in one room for long periods. That way, he could conserve whatever little energy he had. But by evening, the happy aroma of food cooking would enter his nose, and he would be lost. He tried to resist it, but not for long. It was his good luck that the children did not try to catch him in the kitchen. They were probably scared of their mother. And the whole happy drill would begin again. Xoxo would sing in his nasal sing-song voice, directing everybody. It was all make-believe–nobody heard him, and nobody saw him. It was very convenient to Xoxo (Xoxo did not know that his name was Xoxo, else he would have been angry if anybody could see or hear him). It was here that Xoxo was the happiest. He would inhale the lovely smells of the food and then say, 'Neelam, the biryani is very delicious, but don't give the children too much; let them finish their first serve, then serve them again.' Or 'Cylinder, chew your food properly and don't drink too much water in between.' Xoxo's list was endless. He would conduct the whole drama as a military drill without anybody knowing.

After days of tripping over the threads, Xoxo decided he would select a corner for himself and stay there for

most of the time or till the pests went off to sleep. He searched for a quiet corner, but there was no place where the children did not go. It was true that they did not sit anywhere longer than ten minutes, but even that disturbed Xoxo. Finally, he realised that a corner of the large sofa was comparatively free after Hemant left. Hemant would sit there in the morning sipping his tea and reading the newspapers. After that, it would be free till the next day. Plus, there was the charm of reading the newspapers. Xoxo had still not mastered the art of picking up the newspaper. It was because he had no strength. So, he decided to go to the kitchen, where Neelam would make the breakfast, smell the good food and get stronger. That gave him strength for the next two hours or so.

So, the next day, he kept peeping from the upstairs lobby to check whether Hemant had left. His knees hurt from his fall at midnight while trying to come down the stairs. The imps had tied even the balustrade with the thread. He would have fallen headlong on the ground had he not been mentally prepared. Therefore, he controlled himself when he stumbled and floated down the stairs. But his ego got hurt. Because of the pest Cylinder and his peskier sister Opal, he could not roam in his own house as and when he wanted. Now, he also had to be careful about the time. Hence, here he was, finding the right time to find a place for himself to sit and just be.

Finally, Hemant left, and Neelam went to her room

for her bath. In the living room, the obnoxious children were busy doing some craft project for their school. The time and the place seemed quite safe for Xoxo to sit on the sofa and try to pick up the newspaper and read it.

The wind played a very crucial role in his (dead) life. There had been occasions when he had been successful in picking up the newspaper, but for some reason, Neelam always kept the window near the sofa open. She liked the soft, cold wind coming from the window whenever she sat there. Xoxo knew he could pick up the newspaper with just a little practice. But almost all the time, the wind had destroyed his hope of reading the newspaper. It was not a nasty wind which came inside, just a gentle breeze, but it was enough to uproot Xoxo. Xoxo was very kind-hearted when he was alive. Even now, as a ghost, his nature remained kind and soft-hearted. He could not eat the things which ghosts were supposed to eat. He had tried once, but he gagged on it. After that, he did not try anymore. As a result, he was always weak and feeble. Even the gentlest of breeze could blow him to a distance.

Little did he know that the imps had laid a careful trap for him and were play-acting in the corner of the room.

***

Paint the Town Red

In reality, the kids were anxiously waiting for Xoxo to come and sit on the sofa and pick up the newspaper their father had carelessly thrown in the cane basket. They ran to the basket as their father left and put the fresh newspaper underneath the painted newspapers. They had painted only some parts of the paper where a person would touch to pick it.

So off went Xoxo jauntily to the sofa and sat down. He took a minute to settle down and realign his centre of gravity, hoping not to get toppled. Then he bent down to pick up the newspaper. Disaster was waiting to strike the unsuspecting Xoxo, and it did. He had not touched a newspaper for a very long time. So, when it felt slippery in his hands, he didn't pay much attention to it. But the same slipperiness helped him to pick up the newspaper or at least a part of it. But because it was painted, it stuck to his fingers.

On the opposite side of the room, the brother-sister duo was waiting with bated breath. They saw the fluttering and heard the rustle of the newspaper. They could not see Xoxo as he was a ghost and was transparent. But they had seen him as a shadow. By the time Xoxo realised what was happening, it was too late.

The paint stuck to his hand, and so did the paper. He used his other hand to free himself from the newspaper, but the more he shook his hand, the more the paint stuck. Xoxo was scared now. He did not have enough strength to rip the paper from his hands. He saw a movement from the corner of his eye. He looked up and saw Cylinder and Opal coming cautiously towards him. He was so frightened that he could not even move.

He saw the children coming towards him with a tablecloth. Xoxo panicked with fear. Somehow, he gathered whatever little was left of his strength, stood up and ran towards the back wall. The newspaper stuck to his hands, but he did not know it. The only thought in his anxious mind was to escape one way or the other. But when he reached the wall and tried to cross, the newspaper stopped him from going inside the wall.

Xoxo began whimpering with fear. He was sure the children would capture him in the tablecloth and make him a prisoner. He could not allow that. Xoxo pushed himself through the wall. It did not strike him that he could run out from the back door, too. But he was so used to walking through anywhere in the house, door, window, wall, or furniture that he did not think of this practical solution in his panic. Had he been alone, he would have just glided through the wall, but the newspaper stuck to him, and it was creating such a ruckus. Xoxo was crazy with fear now. He had never been so scared in his life or now after death. He tried with all his strength to go through the wall. Ultimately, the paper gave in. He yanked it so hard that the newspaper tore. Xoxo flew through the wall and disappeared. He did not realise that some newspaper shreds were still glued to his finger. The children saw him escaping. They ran after him, but he almost flew and went inside the jungle. The children could not do anything. They were not allowed in the jungle.

'Oh my God, bhaiya, we would have caught him!' Opal exclaimed excitedly.

'Yes, but then what? Ghosts are supposed to kill people and do bad things to them. It is good that we did not catch him. We have to scare him away from our house,' Shailendra was a practical boy. He did not make decisions in a hurry. Even at this young age, he thought before taking any decision. The good thing was when he spoke in this tone, Opal heard him.

'Bhaiya, it ran away in the jungle, but bits of the newspaper were attached to its hand. If they stay glued to his hand, we will know where he is in our house. Then we can scare it away.'

Shailendra nodded in agreement, 'I wonder what it eats and what else he does apart from scaring people.'

'But, bhaiya, he wasn't scaring us or trying to harm us. He was trying to read the newspaper. Now we know he wanders from one room to another without disturbing anybody.'

Shailendra kept quiet. It was true. Xoxo never tried to scare them. Shailendra felt that Xoxo just wanted the freedom to roam about in the house and he wanted to be left alone. But how could they allow this? Their home had to be ghost-free. You never know when Xoxo will become destructive. He wanted to chase away Xoxo right now. The only problem was that he had already run away.

From that day onward, there was no sign of Xoxo anywhere in the house. The threads on the doors were intact, and there was no movement near the sofa or the newspapers. Opal was disappointed. It was all so exciting, and now the ghost was gone, probably never to return.

Xoxo, the ghost, on the other hand, had problems of his own. Only he knew the pain of being chased out of his own home. He dared not to return as the wicked children might have planned something else too. But he was so badly hurt–mentally, emotionally, and physically. He sat on a tree stump in the jungle, nursing his wound. As a ghost, he could not get hurt physically. He was just like the free wind, maybe just a bit thicker. But now, with bits of the newspaper stuck to

his fingers, he stood out like a sore thumb. Not that anybody noticed him. Even if they had, they would have just seen bits of paper floating in the air and not give it another thought.

'I am never going to that house again,' Xoxo thought vehemently, 'I am going to stay here forever in this jungle.' So here was the problem. Xoxo was not the usual ghost who got his sustenance and strength from killing living things and drinking their blood. He was not vicious at all. Whatever little strength he had was only through smells and sounds. He was becoming comfortable in the house with Neelam's cooking. The sounds and the smell of her cooking sent him to another happy world. Not that he ate anything or even wanted to eat, but his senses had become so sharp that these smells and sounds gave him strength and energy.

Xoxo was gradually weakening. He knew that very soon, he was going to die. Die? But he was already dead. Well, something would happen to him if he did not get nourishment immediately. He was too weak to go to the kitchen in the house, but somehow, he dragged himself to the kitchen window. He dared not go inside. He took a deep breath. The chicken curry was bubbling in a big pot, and Neelam was drizzling desi ghee over the parathas. 'Oh, the aroma!' Sitting on the table was Opal, trying to assemble the salad. She was not allowed to use a knife as yet. Her mother had cut the salad ingredients while she was assembling them. Red, juicy, thick tomato slices over the green

salad leaves. Thin rounds of onion and radish came next. The radishes were small round balls with bright red outer covering and white insides. Xoxo remembered that these were slightly less pungent than the usual white radishes but equally crunchy and tasty. Next, she squeezed lemon juice over the salad, drop by drop. Nobody heard the sound, but Xoxo did. He was very fond of salad when he was alive. He loved to eat the lettuce leaves; they were his favourite, especially when sprinkled with salt, pepper, and lime juice. It was the most basic of salads, but just watching Opal assembling it, gave him strength.

Gradually, it became a habit. Xoxo would come and stand near the kitchen window during dinner time and inhale the heady aromas of the delicious food Neelam cooked regularly. It did not give him as much energy as when he was inside and sitting on the dining table, but still, it gave him enough strength to go about with whatever life he had.

In this scenario came Krish–Krish bhaiya was their cousin. He had just turned teen and was fully pompous about it. He looked down on anyone under fourteen as low-class, demented bugs who did not have brains. There was a shadow of light black hair on his upper lip, and his forehead was full of small pimples that neither grew nor disappeared. He was a lanky fourteen-year-old and a cricket buff.

Though Krish sometimes behaved arrogantly, his occasional gentleness made both Opal and Shailendra hero-worship him. Krish looked like a warrior–always alert and ever ready to move and attack. This was probably because Krish bhaiya's favourite dress was his army jacket and cap worn front to back, which was his trademark.

Krish got away with almost everything because he was good in his studies. This does not mean he did not get into any scraps. He did, many times. But almost everybody overlooked it because he was so well-mannered too with the adults. But this time, Krish bhaiya had tried his parents' patience to the limit. He brought a pup to keep in their house. His friend's bitch had given birth to two puppies. One they were keeping, and the other they were donating to anyone who wanted it. Krish bhaiya's friend Naresh did not want to give the pup to anybody. He wanted it to be well looked after. It was not a difficult desire.

Anyone who is a dog-lover would have fallen in love with the pup. It was a mixed breed, a cross between a Maltese and a Beagle, and God knows what else. But it was the cutest pup in the world. Krish bhaiya considered himself above the coochi cooing of babies or animals. But he was an animal-loving boy and had already fallen in love with the pup. What was not there to love in it? It had silky golden brown fur with a few white patches and a small black patch on its left side. But the best part was its limpid dark brown eyes that had just opened a few days back. It looked at you so trustingly, and if you went too near it, a small pink tongue would come out and lick you with affection. Its nose was still pink. Krish bhaiya didn't know whether it would become brown or black as it grew up. Because the pup was a mixture of many colours and species, Krish bhaiya named it Chutney. So, Chutney it was.

Krish bhaiya's parents had to go outstation for a wedding. Krish didn't want to go. His mother was also secretly relieved. She knew Krish would have been very uncomfortable there. They would have had to leave Chutney behind. Krish was looking forward to his holidays with his cousins. He wanted to spend time with his cousins Shailendra and Opal, who revered even the ground he walked on. The arrangement suited both Krish and his parents.

Krish wanted to come here as he had heard so much about this large house near the jungle. He wanted to explore the jungle, too. So here he was with his young pet Chutney. His parents dropped Krish at Hemant uncle's house and left after some time. Though Shailendra was neutral, Opal immediately fell in love with the puppy, and vice versa. Though Chutney was Krish's dog, he became Opal's, too. A deep bond of love developed between the two. Chutney was always in Opal's arms now. Krish was happy, too, as now he could explore the jungle freely. It would take some time for Chutney to begin barking or growling, though protecting his people was ingrained in him. At present, he was getting lots and lots of love, precisely what a pup needs.

The jungle was another matter altogether. Now that Krish bhaiya was here, their mother, Neelam, allowed them to explore the jungle a bit more. It helped that Krish bhaiya's parents gave him a mobile phone for emergencies.

So, off they went along with Krish, Shailendra and Opal with Chutney in her arms. Chutney was too young to trot along their side. He slept most of the time, waking just enough to drink the bottled milk and stretch his legs. Shailendra was holding a picnic basket. Their mother had given them a sumptuous picnic basket full of sandwiches, fried chicken, grapes, strawberries and fruit juices. Krish had directed Opal to keep some bottled milk for Chutney. Opal was more than happy to look after Chutney.

Going inside the jungle was like watching a 5D movie. There were so many shades of green, from the lightest to the darkest. There were many kinds of insects; some they recognised, others they did not. They saw red-coloured beetles with flecks of black dots on their outer covering. There were red, brown, and green shrubs. There was one tree that stood out among the other trees and shrubs. It was a huge tree. It was a tall tree and equally broad too. Krish bhaiya knew what it was. It had oval-shaped green leaves, and was covered with reddish, pinkish fruit flecked with white patches. The majestic tree was full of lush green leaves and reddish fruits. The fruits looked different from the usual ones. They looked like the sweet mithai Jalebi, a round concoction fried in oil and then soaked in sugar syrup. It looked like a cross between Jalebi and the tamarind fruit. Except that it looked much better than both Jalebi and the Tamarind fruit. The fruits had knots like the French beans, although thicker and both the ends curled towards

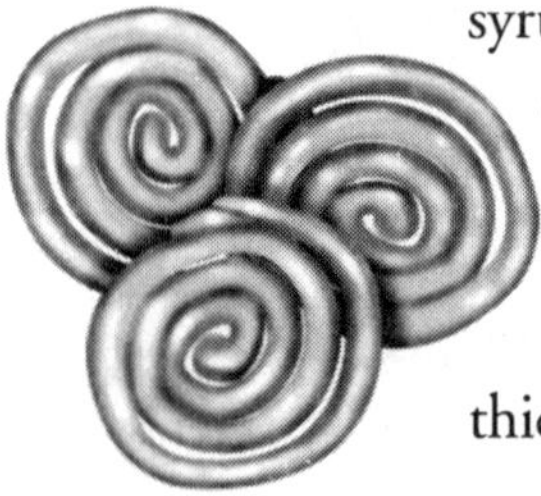

each other. There must be thousands of fruits dangling on the tree. In their imagination, they even saw the fruits twinkling. It looked like a magical tree in front of a witch's house.

Opal looked around, but of course, there was no house or cottage, nor were they scared. Everyone knows that when you are scared, you also feel the atmosphere changing and becoming dark, and sometimes you hear blood-curdling sounds. But nothing of this sort was happening, so they knew that they were in a safe place.

'I know what it is,' Krish bhaiya declared, 'It is called Jungle Jalebi because of how it looks,' saying so he plucked some fruit from the tree and began peeling it.

'Careful, bhaiya, it might be poisonous.'

'No, it's not poisonous at all. I ate quite a lot of it when I went to Chennai. It is one of the tastiest fruits. See,' Krish put the fruit in his mouth and began chewing it. Then he spat out the seed, 'Here, have some, you two, we don't get to eat Jungle Jalebi often. These trees are not very common on our side.'

Gingerly, they took the fruit from Krish bhaiya, peeled it and ate it. It was good, sweet, less sour than tamarind and crunchy like an apple. It was a new but tasty fruit. They plucked a few more of the Jungle Jalebis and ate them. Chutney, too, wanted to eat, but he was too small.

What made the jungle awesome was a stream running through a part of it. Leaves, moss, and broken branches were carelessly floating in it, but as far as they could see, its water was as clear as crystal. Krish led them to the spring, and they drank its sweet and cool water. The whole place was not a jungle. It was like farms interspersed with it. Sometimes, they saw miles and miles of paddy carpets and then the jungle again. After the jungles, there were some low-height mountains.

'We'll come for hiking tomorrow,' Krish declared. The others nodded happily. They would do whatever Krish bhaiya said.

'Let's eat now, bhaiya,' all of them were hungry by now, Shailendra more so, as he was carrying the picnic hamper. They cleared a space around a broken tree trunk. It was just the height to be used as a table. Opal put down Chutney, who was becoming a bit impatient now. She took out the food items and set the table. The aroma of the food made them hungrier. Quickly, they washed their hands and sat down to eat.

All the running and walking had made them quite hungry and thirsty. Their mother cooked well; she had packed the picnic hamper with great care and love. They wolfed down the cheese sandwiches and the fried chicken drumsticks and drank their fruit juices.

Opal had put Chutney on the sheet she had brought for him. It was when they sat down after the delicious meal that Opal noticed two strange things. One was that Chutney was attempting to wag his tail. He was too young to wag, but he seemed to be shaking it happily. He was also repeatedly taking out his tiny, pink tongue as if he wanted to lick a piece of paper floating there. Why would Chutney try to lick paper? Wait! Opal squinted her eyes and looked closely at the paper bit. She picked up Chutney in her arms and tried catching the paper bit. Chutney was happy and gave her a small lick.

Opal stretched out her hand and tried to catch the paper. To her surprise, it immediately floated above. Opal was surprised. There was no wind. She tried to reach it again. Again, the paper floated out of her reach. A thought struck her mind. She was shocked. She looked at Shailendra and Krish bhaiya. Both were busy whittling a piece of wood. Krish was teaching him how to carve with a knife.

'Bhaiya,' Opal called out. Both of them did not hear her.

'Bhaiya,' she was more insistent now. Shailendra heard the nervousness in her voice. He looked at her. Krish was still whittling the piece of wood.

'What?'

'See the bit of paper bhaiya?'

Shailendra looked around. There was a small piece of paper in the air. It looked like a torn newspaper. Something clicked with him as well. Could it be? No, it can't be. He looked at Opal. She nodded, then whispered, 'The newspaper we had put the paint on. Some of it must have stuck to his hand. Bhaiya, I think it is Xoxo. But what is he doing here? I thought it hated us, especially after the paint incident.'

Shailendra was equally confused. The piece of paper was not dangling in the air just like that. It seemed to be walking from one place to another. It even went far from them once but came back and hovered near them.

The piece of newspaper was indeed stuck to Xoxo's fingers. He did not have the strength to pull it off. He was stuck with it till the time the paper weakened and dropped. We know Xoxo was unlike the other ghosts, always scaring and sometimes killing people. Xoxo was here because he was a friendly ghost, and he liked company, not much, just a bit to make him smile. A good company also gave him energy. Although the children had made him miserable in the house, he had developed a liking for them. It was an 'On-Off' relationship–now he liked them, now he did not. At present, he did not like them. Instead, he was cursing them because, in their own way, they had chased him out of his house. Moreover, he had annoying bits of the newspaper glued to his hand. One good thing about being a ghost was that he could glide and float anywhere without any hindrances. But now, even with such a small piece of paper glued to his hand, he could not float freely.

But after a week outside in the jungle, he had neither energy nor good company. He had begun missing the pests. There, he could at least see and hear them. That and the aroma of good food kept him in a jovial and happy mood. So he was surprised when he caught their smell in this part of the jungle. Xoxo knew that Shailendra and Opal were not allowed to come this far in the jungle. Yet, he became fearful again.

Together with the smell of these two smells, there was a mixture of other smells. One was a neutral smell, just a bit negative. But the other made all the difference. It was such a happy and trusting smell. Cautiously, he

went near them. There was another, slightly older boy, with them. He did not seem to be a problem, but Xoxo was not taking any chances. He had learnt through experience to stay away from young boys. So, where was the happy smell coming from? He looked around. There it was. A small pup in Opal's arm, partly sleeping, partly awake.

The puppy opened its eyes, and their eyes met. Chutney smiled, or that was what Xoxo thought. Xoxo melted at the sight of the beautiful, happy puppy. On his part, Chutney did not know the difference between a man and a human being. He just saw a man who would give him lots of love. Xoxo cautiously went near the pup and tried to touch it. The pup opened its eyes, saw Xoxo, smiled, and then licked him with his small pink tongue. Xoxo was shocked. For the first time since his death, he felt the touch of another living being. He liked it. This time, he softly patted the pup's head. Chutney licked him again. Xoxo almost did a happy dance in front of the pup. Chutney would have happily barked if he knew how to bark. That would come later on after he grew up a little. The loving lick had given Xoxo enough energy to last him a few hours.

The children were now sitting down for lunch. Xoxo was hovering around. The delicious aroma of the food reached him. Xoxo closed his eyes with enjoyment. He knew Neelam had cooked all this–the fried chicken, cheese sandwich, vegetable cutlets and fruit juices. It was a tasty treat for the children but not for Xoxo. For Xoxo, it was manna from heaven; it was life, or in Xoxo's case, we can say it was a means of survival.

Since his soul did not allow him to live in the cruel ways of the other ghosts or other such creatures, his sense of smell had developed to such a great extent that he could continue living as a ghost for a long time. It was as if when he smelled the food, it actually turned into nutrition for his mind and body. That is how he got his energy and strength. And now, the unconditional love and trust from the pup gave him more energy. Xoxo could now walk and even run. For the first time in his life after death, he felt truly happy. He kept hovering in the hope of smelling more yummy food and maybe getting a few extra licks from the pup, whose name, he learnt, was Chutney.

But as everyone knows, happiness does not last long. And the same happened with Xoxo, too. The piece from the newspaper was still glued to his hand. Opal noticed it and was immediately suspicious. When she was sure it was indeed Xoxo, she became alert and yet excited. She had been feeling guilty from the time Xoxo fled from their house in terror.

That was not her intention. She just wanted to show Shailendra bhaiya that there was indeed a ghost in their new house. Bhaiya was convinced, but Xoxo did not return. They had scared him away with the newspaper and paint.

Opal was one hundred per cent sure that the bit of paper floating around them was Xoxo. She looked at

Shailendra bhaiya and Krish bhaiya. Shailendra bhaiya was also alert on seeing the floating piece of newspaper.

'What are you two staring at?' Krish bhaiya had looked up. Shailendra and Opal looked at each other, unsure what to say to Krish bhaiya. Krish bhaiya was their role model. It would be wrong to hide anything from Krish bhaiya. But how could they tell him about this almost harmless and friendly ghost? Though Chutney was very young, he was trying to wag his tail at the piece of paper and even gave it a lick. They all knew how much dogs knew about good and bad people and things. Opal made her mind to speak to Krish bhaiya, 'Krish bhaiya, promise you will not tell anyone!'

'Huh! What? What should I not tell anyone?' he smiled, 'First, I have to know before I keep the secret.'

***

Word in the Woods

'Okay, bhaiya,' Opal spoke softly, 'You see that piece of paper?' she pointed to the floating paper.

'What? Paper? Oh, you mean this small paper floating in the wind?'

'Yes, bhaiya, but there is no wind.' Krish looked around. The jungle was shining. It had rained a few hours back and the leaves, trees and shrubs looked fresh, green and happy. But did a shadow cross the jungle? Did the jungle become dull for a few moments? Krish blinked his eyes. The jungle looked fine again. Krish stretched out his hand to catch the paper, but as soon as his hands reached it, it flew some distance away. Krish went after it again, this time more swiftly, but the small piece of paper dodged him again. Krish was embarrassed now. His cousins looked up to him as their idols. And here, he could not catch a piece of paper.

'Krish bhaiya,' Shailendra spoke now, 'It's not just a piece of paper. It's something else.'

Krish looked at them unbelievingly. He was flustered and red-faced. So when Shailendra explained, he jumped at it.

'So tell me, what is it?' Krish was being gentle with Shailendra. Opal looked at them. She could make out that Krish bhaiya was not going to believe Shailendra. She would have to take matters into her own hands now.

'Krish bhaiya, come let us sit down. Chutney is squirming. He wants to stretch his legs,' she delicately put Chutney on the mossy ground. Chutney looked around with half-closed eyes, yawned, and stretched his legs and body. Then, seeing that the others were not in the mood to pick him up again, he curled up on the mat Opal had unrolled for him and promptly went to sleep again.

'Bhaiya,' Opal began hesitatingly, 'That is not a piece of paper. It is a piece of paper, but attached to a body, the body of a ghost.'

For a moment, Krish was not sure he had heard her right. Then he smiled, 'Oh Oppie, for a moment, I thought it was something serious. Where did you get the idea that this piece of paper was attached to a moving ghost?' he demanded and pulled her cheek.

Opal and Shailendra knew they had a task ahead, but they were not giving up. Krish bhaiya had come here for his holidays, and they had to have him on their side. Xoxo was a big secret. Even Opal and Shailendra didn't know whether Xoxo was a good or bad ghost. They just knew that he wasn't harmful. He might be good because Opal thought she saw Chutney licking the air, which meant he might be licking Xoxo. She knew that dogs knew from inside when a person was good or bad. So, her guess was that Xoxo was a good ghost.

Now, to convince Krish bhaiya to believe them, she slowly told Krish bhaiya the whole story–about the small piece of glass she had found, through which she had seen Xoxo for the first time. Then she told him about Xoxo wanting to read the newspaper and their paint episode. In the beginning, Krish did not pay attention to the story, because he knew that Opal was a good storyteller. Then, gradually, Krish bhaiya became serious. He smiled when he heard about the paint incident and them painting the trunk of trees so Neelam Aunty wouldn't suspect them.

Krish mussed Shailendra's hair, 'Cylinder,' Krish teased him, 'Do you also believe this?'

'Yes, bhaiya, I saw Xoxo's hand glued to the paper and Xoxo trying to escape. He panicked because he could pass through the wall, but the paper could not.'

'So you have given him a name, too,' Krish laughed.

Shailendra smiled, 'It was Opal's idea. We can change it if you want.'

'No, not really, but first, I have to affirm whether there is really a ghost. But if there is a ghost, then, why didn't Chutney show his discomfort even though he is too young to bark?'

'Bhaiya, Chutney licked Xoxo!' Opal exclaimed, 'That is why you see the small piece of newspaper hovering around us because Chutney was licking him happily.'

'But I have to see him myself before I believe him. And as you say, he is transparent, so you had to paint the newspaper to catch him. We will have to do something like that again.'

'Xoxo will not easily come to the house again.'

'Bhaiya,' Opal addressed both of them, 'Let's see if we can talk to him.'

'What?' both the brothers turned to her in surprise, 'How will you do that?'

Opal turned to Shailendra, 'Bhaiya, remember when Xoxo was trying to escape with the newspaper stuck on him, he was banging on the wall. A clapping sound would come out as his hands touched the wall. I think, if we talk to him and ask him to answer by clapping, then Krish bhaiya will know that he is really there.'

'But how will we find him?'

'Bhaiya, I'm sure that Xoxo is here. For this, we have to look carefully at Chutney when he tries to wag his tail or lick a piece of paper. We have to be alert as the paper is becoming smaller and might disappear soon. Then, if we see these signs, we will try to talk to Xoxo.'

Krish was hesitant, but there was no other solution either. So, they waited. In the meantime, Opal fed milk to Chutney from a bottle. Suddenly, Shailendra sat up. The others looked at him. Sure enough, there was now a tiny piece of paper floating near Chutney, and he seemed to be enjoying it by jumping a bit. Then Chutney took out his small pink tongue and licked the air.

Krish was now completely engrossed in it. He now believed Opal's story. Chutney could see the ghost, and he liked it, too. Krish looked at Opal and Shailendra. Shailendra gestured to Opal, 'Speak to it, Opal.'

Opal nodded and turned towards Chutney. Chutney had his face up as if he was looking at something or someone. She began, 'My name is Opal, and these are my brothers. We want to be friends with you. Can you hear me?'

The newspaper fragment became still momentarily, then started going away from them.

'Wait, please wait, don't go, we won't harm you. The other day, when you got the paint on your fingers, we didn't want to scare you, we just wanted to see you. We're sorry. If we had known that you would get hurt we would never have done it.' Without wanting to, Opal began crying. Shailendra and Krish, hardly breathing, waited. They saw the bit of paper stop its movement as if it heard Opal, and then it came near. Opal sniffed, but she had her plan ready, 'I know you cannot speak, or even if you do, we cannot hear you. But I think you can clap. If this is so, can you please clap once for yes and two claps for no?'

There was a long moment. Even the jungle had heard Opal's request and waited, with bated breath, for Xoxo to answer. There was total silence everywhere. The very air had become still. There was a pin-drop silence. Even the trilling insects were waiting.

At last, after a long wait, the paper floated towards them, and there was a muffled clap. It was like a soft clap when someone is wearing gloves. The jungle sighed,

birds and the insects began chattering again. The wind started moving, and the leaves sang. The three children heaved a sigh of relief.

After that, there was a flurry of questions and answers. They would ask questions one after another, and Xoxo would answer them either with one clap or two. After ten minutes or so, they began enjoying themselves. But there were so many things that did not have a straight answer; they required some explanations. Like, 'When did you become a ghost, or when did you die?' A clap wouldn't have answered them. So, they tried reframing their questions.

'Did you die in our house?' One clap.

'Did somebody kill you?' their eyes widened when there was one clap.

'Where was your house?' no answer.

'Where is your family?' there was no answer because the answer required more than one or two claps.

After some time, even these claps stopped.

'Xoxo, are you there?' no answer.

'I think he has become weak. Is it so, Xoxo?' Opal asked him. There was a barely muted clap. They had to strain their ears to hear him. Krish and Shailendra took the last pieces of the fried chicken drumsticks and began eating while they waited for Xoxo to clap. There was complete silence from Xoxo. They had an inkling that Xoxo had become very weak. Krish and Shailendra went near Xoxo.

Opal was already there. It was where they thought Xoxo would be. They traced him again when Chutney licked the air near him, he was now leaning against something they could not see. Chutney had curled up there and gone to sleep. Krish and Shailendra still had their fried chicken in their hands. They went and sat near Chutney and observed him. Suddenly, they heard a muffled clap. It was Xoxo.

'Xoxo!' Opal exclaimed, 'Are you hungry?' a muffled clap again.

'Here, you can have this chicken drumstick,' Shailendra stretched his hands with the chicken snack. Xoxo did not take it from him, but, after some time, they felt he was a bit nourished. Chutney had woken up and had begun licking the air again. But though Xoxo did not eat the chicken, he had somehow got his strength. They were perplexed. Suddenly, Opal blurted out, 'I think he got his strength from the smell of the chicken. Is it so Xoxo?' There was a clap, one clap, which meant 'yes.'

Krish did not need more conviction, 'Here, smell my fried chicken too,' he stretched out his hand to where he thought Xoxo would be sitting or lying.

'Here take mine too,' even Shailendra hurriedly stretched his arm towards where he thought Xoxo was. They waited in anticipation. Were they thinking right? They had a hazy idea that ghosts were scary; they frightened and killed people and were very strong as they killed people and animals and ate them. So, how could this ghost be different from the other ghosts? Ghosts were ghosts; there were no categories. So how could

Xoxo be a weak ghost, revived just by the smell of good-cooked food? But that is what seemed to be happening now. They waited in suspense for Xoxo to get a good smell of their food. It seemed to have an effect, as after some time, the newspaper piece began dancing in front of them, even when there was no breeze.

'Xoxo, have you got your energy back?'

There was a strong clap.

'Do you need to smell some more or want to eat this piece of chicken?' Opal offered him her piece. There were two vehement claps, which meant 'No.'

'Tell us something more about yourself, Xoxo,' Krish asked. They waited for his answer. They waited for some time, then realised that Xoxo could not speak; he could respond only with clapping. They would have to ask 'Yes' or 'No' questions that Xoxo would reply with one or two claps.

Opal looked around. It was getting dark. Their mother had told them to return before dark. Chutney had finished all his milk and would be hungry after some time. Though Opal was the youngest in this group, she was more practical than the others.

'Bhaiya, I think we should go back now. Mummy had instructed us to return by evening.'

'Yes, we will go back now, but how can we leave Xoxo here? He'll be lonely here, and we may not find him here the next time.'

Even Krish looked undecided.

Opal thought for a minute, then exclaimed, 'Let us ask Xoxo if he will come with us. He used to stay in our house earlier,' Opal turned towards Xoxo, 'Xoxo, we have to go back. Please come along with us to our home, your home. We assure you that we will not do silly things to you anymore. Let us be friends.'

There was no sound, no clap. There was silence all around. The living beings of the jungle, too, waited for a reply. The jungle didn't want Xoxo to leave. He was a gentle soul, unlike the other ghouls who hung to the branches using them as swings and stopped them from growing upward or sideways. They munched on the tiny creatures, crushed them ruthlessly under their feet, and sometimes picked them up by the fist, half chewing them and spitting them out. Xoxo was not like that at all. For all purposes, Xoxo was a vegan ghost who did not eat, just smelled. The smell just gave him enough strength to move about.

***

Welcome Home, Xoxo!

After a long wait, during which Xoxo considered all the pros and cons of returning to his home, he decided he would give the children one more chance. Xoxo was unfamiliar with Krish, but he wanted to return home so badly that he agreed to go with them. Hence there was one clap.

The children were waiting for it. They whooped in delight and clapped, too. Opal picked up Chutney. The boys packed up the rest of the things, and everybody started back home. In between, they checked whether Xoxo was with them or not. Sure enough, he was. They could make out by the small piece of newspaper floating merrily alongside them.

They rushed inside noisily. 'Hello, children, had a

good time?' Neelam asked them though she could figure out that the day had gone well for them. They were dirty but happy. After washing her hands, Opal immediately warmed up some milk for Chutney, who was famished. He slurped over his milk bottle.

'Go and have your bath, children. Dinner is almost ready.'

'Chachi, I have brought something for you,' saying this, Krish took out a few Jungle Jalebis from his pocket and gave them to Neelam.

Neelam was surprised, 'What are these? Oh, wait! I know, these are Jungle Jalebis. Is there a Jungle Jalebi tree in the jungle? I had them when I was small. It is a rare tree. It doesn't grow much on our side in North India.'

'Yes, Chachi, there is a huge tree. We ate a few and I got these for you.'

'Thank you, beta,' Neelam patted him on the head. Then she washed one fruit and put it in her mouth.

'Delicious!' she exclaimed, 'Reminds me of my school days. Now go, all of you. Dinner will be ready in half an hour.'

They rushed to their rooms, but not before Opal noticed a piece of paper fluttering near the dining table where Neelam was already putting the food. Opal smiled to herself. Xoxo was going to get plenty of energy today.

One of the reasons that their food was always so delicious and full of aroma was that Neelam was an excellent cook and she cooked for her family with love. She loved her family like any other mother and housewife. Her love went into her food and the little ways in which she cared for her house and family. Often, she also liked to experiment with other cuisines.

Tonight, they were having Palak Paneer, Aloo Gobhi, Jeera rice, chapatis, curd and salad. For dessert, they would have coconut laddus. What was there not to like? Neelam was happy that though the children did not like spinach, they loved Palak Paneer. But the person most excited here was, no doubt, Xoxo. He loved the crackling of cumin seed in ghee and the aroma just before she added rice. There was another aroma coming out when she sauteed the rice. This heavenly smell was enough to give Xoxo energy to last two days. There were so many delicious treats. Somehow, Neelam had made every item different from the others. There was no mixing of either taste or smell. Xoxo was in his seventh heaven.

The first thing that the children did after coming down from their baths was to search for Xoxo. Sure enough, he was there, almost dancing on the opposite chair where nobody sat unless there were more people. But the fragment of paper glued to his hand had become so small that they had to look for it. Good in a way that their mother would not notice it. But Opal was worried that once the paper falls off, how would they know if Xoxo was with them? She looked at Shailendra. He was also looking a bit worried. Maybe he was thinking the same, but Opal wasn't sure. After that, there was a lot of chewing and chomping. They had enjoyed their food and were now polishing off the coconut laddus. Neelam had made them with fresh coconut and clotted cream, and they were delicious. Xoxo's mouth watered as soon the smell of fresh coconut reached his nostrils. He inhaled deeply. He now had so much energy that he felt he could even talk. But nothing happened. He did not even try too hard. Plenty of time for that, maybe tomorrow or the day after, or any other day. Today, Xoxo was just happy with the energy surcharge. He had become like a starving street dog in the last few days. But now he was so happy and energetic that he wanted to dance. And dance he did on the chair he had allocated to himself.

They went upstairs to their bedrooms. Krish and Shailendra were sharing Shailendra's bedroom, while Opal was in her bedroom beside her parents'. Xoxo wanted to stay back and smell some more of the great food. He reluctantly went behind the children. But, no issues, he had enough strength to last him almost three to four days. At present, there was such a surge of energy in Xoxo that he was not only following the children, but he was also running, no, he was floating ahead of them, then tripping over the balustrade, falling, picking himself, and then, again running ahead of them. Krish was also there with them, but Opal and Shailendra noticed it more. Both of them were happy to see Xoxo happy. However, it did surprise them that Xoxo was behaving with such childlike glee. 'Had he been a child when he was alive?' Opal wondered. 'I'll ask him later,' she said to herself, 'he may not like to talk about it now.'

Xoxo was so happy to get his energy back that he kept jumping around. Suddenly, Xoxo disappeared; the piece of the newspaper glued to his finger was lying on the floor motionless. Krish discovered this.

'Look, Xoxo has either fallen or escaped!' he exclaimed.

'Why should he escape, bhaiya?' Opal questioned, 'We did not imprison him. He came because he wanted to. He was so happy just now and was jumping on the stairs. Xoxo! Are you here? Has anything happened? Are you lying on the ground?'

'Shh! Not so loudly, mummy will hear. She may come up too.'

Opal lowered her voice, 'Xoxo if the paper has come out, give us a sign that you are here. I know you are here.'

There were a few muffled claps. They all heaved sighs of relief. Suddenly, there was a flurry of movement on Shailendra's study table. Apart from his books and copies, there were many things on it. Shailendra was very fond of pens; he spent all his pocket money on pens. Knowing this, his parents had presented him with a pen many times. Apart from that, there were his games and gadgets, too, though these were kept on a separate table. It was here in his collection of pens that there were some unnatural movements. Shailendra's prized ink pen stood vertically as if it wanted to do a jig. They all waited to see what was going to happen. They had guessed correctly. It was Xoxo who had picked up the pen!

On his side, Xoxo was ecstatic! To have the strength to hold a pen! It was unbelievable!

He could pick up the pen. He was so fond of writing when he was alive. In his spare time, he used to write about the history of India and the world. He frantically looked around for a paper to write, write something, and write anything! Oh! How wonderful it would be to indulge in his favourite hobby again.

Krish was watching this with awe. Though he was convinced about the presence of this ghost they called Xoxo, he still did not buy into the idea.

'You want a paper to write something, Xoxo?' Krish blurted out, 'Here, take this paper,' he kept a size A4 sheet on the study table and stepped back. Then they waited in suspense for Xoxo to write something. After a long pause, in which Xoxo seemed to adjust the pen in his hand, some squiggly lines did appear on the page. Everyone excitedly craned their heads to see what Xoxo had written. They could not make out anything. It was just a crisscross of shaky lines like they had once seen on a heart monitor of one of their relatives in hospital. Disappointed, they looked at each other.

'These are nothing. These are just zigzag lines without any meaning,' Shailendra was disappointed.

Krish pondered, 'You know, Xoxo must have been a ghost for many years. And he is not a normal ghost, he is a soft ghost with many good human qualities. He gets his strength from inhaling good smells. It is a great achievement that he can even hold a pen. I'm sure Xoxo is trying very hard,' then added loudly, 'Isn't it, Xoxo?' There was no response from Xoxo. He was busy trying to write on the paper. The pen was still quivering. The children waited for some time but then got bored.

'Here,' Krish gave his iPad to Shailendra, 'You have a look at it, I'll use my phone. What about you, Opal?'

'Oh, I'll make some painting, bhaiya,' Opal loved painting and pencil sketching too. Her parents were so proud of her that they gave her anything she wanted for her artwork. She took some papers, brought her pack of pencils, and sat on a small table nearby. Shailendra squealed with delight when Krish bhaiya gave him the iPad. That is why both of them liked Krish bhaiya. He was so large-hearted. He shared everything with them. But Krish did this only with Opal and Shailendra, not with everybody. He liked how they adored him and hung on to his every word. He knew they were his biggest fans, and he returned their feelings. He felt protective towards them. He loved Chutney, and Chutney, too, loved his lopsided caring. It wouldn't have made any difference to Chutney. But it was a relief when Opal took over the upkeep of Chutney. Opal, too, had fallen in love with Chutney and was looking after him in a disciplined manner.

So here they were, all five of them–Krish on the mobile, Shailendra on the iPad, Opal sketching, Xoxo trying to straighten his hand, and Chutney partly sleeping on the carpet. Once in a while, he would open his eyes, yawn, and give a yip, like a small bark. Opal was trying to make a black-and-white sketch of Shailendra bhaiya's study table and an invisible ghost hovering over it. And she was doing a good job. It is a difficult thing to draw an invisible ghost. But Opal was drawing well, with light slashes of her soft grey pencil.

Slowly, they became aware of a muffled sound. It was so soft that initially, they could not hear and pay attention to it. This time, the sound was a little louder. Shailendra looked up. It seemed like Xoxo's clap. And indeed, it was. But it was not what they had agreed upon, one clap for yes and two claps for no. It was a series of soft, muffled claps. Shailendra saw that the pen that Xoxo was using was still in an upright position. He peered at the paper on the table. To his astonishment, there was actually something written on it. Oh! Thought Shailendra, that is why Xoxo wanted our attention. He is holding the pen in one hand and clapping it with the other. That is why the sound was so soft. There were wavy and squiggly lines and figures all over the page as if a spider with ink on his legs had walked over the paper.

'Krish bhaiya, Opal, come here!' he called them urgently. They looked up from their work, saw his expression and rushed towards the table. Not to be left behind, Chutney, too, trotted behind them. Opal gasped. For amongst the squiggles, there was a word, even though it was curly and bumpy. But the word was clear. It was

'HELLO!'

***

Soul That Spells!

'Ooh! Bhaiya! Xoxo can write!' Opal was delighted. Krish and Shailendra were suitably impressed. Opal clapped, and Chutney, too, yipped happily.

'Good work, Xoxo, it must have taken a huge effort to write. Hello, from us too, Xoxo.'

Xoxo wanted to bow to the applause. But a catastrophe struck at that time. He had been holding the pen and practising for so long that now his strength had drained out. The moment he tried to take the bow, the pen clattered to the floor and, along with it, fell Xoxo. Of course, nobody saw Xoxo falling because he was a ghost and was invisible. The bit of newspaper glued to his finger had dropped. They had a general idea that Xoxo might have fallen near the table. He did not clap, or maybe he could not clap.

Opal was the first to comment, 'Bhaiya, I think Xoxo spent all his energy using the pen and trying to write.'

'You're right,' Krish, too, tried to clarify, 'How much energy can one have just by inhaling a good smell?'

'That means if we give him something nice to smell, he might revive after some time,' Shailendra suggested.

'I'll just run to the kitchen pantry and get some biscuits,' Opal jumped up and ran towards the kitchen. She was soon back with some chocolate biscuits and a few Oreos. She kept the chocolate biscuits where she thought Xoxo must have fallen.

'I'm going to crush these Oreos so that he can smell them faster.' Quickly, she put the Oreos on a piece of paper, took a paperweight, crushed them and kept them near the chocolate biscuits. Nothing happened.

'I think if we change the position of the biscuits, Xoxo might be able to smell them easily,' Shailendra suggested.

So they kept changing the place of the biscuits where they thought Xoxo would smell them easily. Their problem was soon easily solved, a solution which they had not thought of. Chutney was there with them in all the hullaballoo. Suddenly, he went under the middle of the study table and began licking the air there.

'Oh! He's there; we were putting the biscuit in the wrong place,' saying this, Opal shifted the page with the biscuit towards where Chutney was sitting happily. Soon, there was a small, muffled clap. They heaved a sigh of relief.

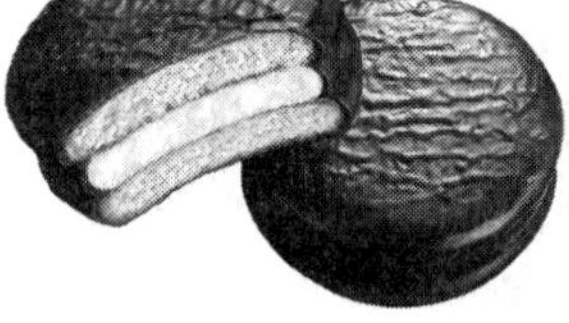

'Welcome, Xoxo,' Krish commented, 'You really scared us. From now on, we'll ensure you always have something good to smell. And Xoxo, there is one more request. Today, we could know your position because of Chutney. But there will be times when Chutney will not be with us. I suggest you again glue a small bit of paper or cloth to your finger so that we will know your position.'

There was a silence as if Xoxo was mulling over this advice. Then there was a small, muffled clap, which meant that Xoxo had agreed to Krish bhaiya's suggestion.

'Give me a piece of cloth,' Krish turned towards Shailendra.

'Yes, bhaiya,' Shailendra rushed towards his almirah, took out one of his handkerchiefs, took a scissor and a fabric glue and gave them to Krish bhaiya. Krish carefully cut a tiny piece of the handkerchief, applied glue to one side and kept it near Xoxo.

'Xoxo put the forefinger of your right hand on this piece of cloth and then let it dry. You have to wave it a few times to dry it.'

After some time, they saw the bit of cloth floating in the air. Relieved, they looked at each other and smiled.

'Thank you, Xoxo, now we will know where you are, and we can help you too. I'll make sure that there is always a cookie or a piece of cake or Kheer or something nice kept around so you can maintain your strength. I think you should relax a bit. After all, you've just recovered.'

The cloth floated around them merrily, then landed on Shailendra's study table. Xoxo was trying to pick up the pen, but he still had not recouped enough to pick up the pen. Opal quickly kept the biscuits on the table. Chutney didn't like it a bit. He had gone to sleep using Xoxo as a pillow. Opal picked him up, so he went to sleep again.

Xoxo was like a ghost in a hurry. He was so excited about being able to do something that he loved when he was alive, which was writing. Ever since he discovered that he was a ghost, which was a great shock to him, he found he could not do things he loved to do when he was alive.

He tried to pick up the pen. It was like picking the heaviest weight. Try as he might, he could not get a hold of it. They could make out that Xoxo was trying very hard because of the bit of cloth glued to his finger.

'Xoxo, you must rest now,' Opal almost ordered him. Xoxo stopped. There was something familiar about the voice. No, not the voice, but the tone. Decades back, his mother used to scold him in this authoritative voice. He was scared of his mother when she spoke to him in this tone, and he always bowed down to this tone. It was the same here, too. He flinched. It was his mother telling him to go to bed. Even now, he could not ignore this tone. He gave up and sat down glumly on the table.

Opal softened her tone. She felt it was a bit harsh, 'Xoxo, I think you can sleep in the next room. It is empty; nobody goes there. There is a bed there too. I'll make it, and place a plate of biscuits there too.'

When Opal spoke in that tone, Xoxo had no option but to follow her. Opal picked up the plate of biscuits and went to the other room. There was a single bed, all made up, but Opal patted it again.

'Off you go to sleep now. I'll leave Chutney with you so that you don't feel alone.' Chutney immediately cuddled up to Xoxo, gave him a few licks, and then went to sleep. The children, too, went to their rooms to sleep.

The next day, Shailendra woke up to some soft scratching sounds. It wasn't a familiar sound. He opened one eye just a bit out of curiosity. He saw his pen standing straight over a paper on his study table. Shailendra turned over to the other side and went off to sleep again. When he woke up after one hour, Krish too had got up. Opal came to their room, 'Xoxo is not there in his room; is he here? There he is!'

Sure enough, the pen was moving in a zigzag pattern all over the paper and sometimes on the study table. She went to the table to look closely at what he had written.

'MY NAME IS PN VERMA.
THIS HOUSE IS MINE.'

It was written in a squiggly manner, one letter up and the other down, some letters were written too far away so that putting it together in a word took some time.

'It can't be your house. Our father took this house far from the town on rent because it charged the lowest. Papa's business had collapsed, so we had to cut down expenses. Nobody was taking this house because people said it was haunted. But Papa and Mummy took it because we don't believe in ghosts,' they all looked at each other and laughed. Yes, nobody believed in ghosts, and here they were conversing with one.

In their way, they started liking Xoxo and felt that Xoxo

liked them too. It was like Xoxo was their very own private secret. They could naturally talk about him to anybody. Another thing they were sure about was that they would have to learn some cooking so that Xoxo could survive, of course, as a ghost. Opal was still too young for her mother to allow her to be independent in the kitchen. Until now, Shailendra had not shown any interest in cooking. That left Krish bhaiya. So, in the garb of spending a part of their time learning how to cook, they would get permission from Neelam aunty or mummy to allow some cooking, like baking, boiling, or making eggs.

When Xoxo regained his strength, he began practicing his writing seriously. Now, they could easily read whatever he wrote. It was introductory, like 'What are your names?' or 'My name is ……, but you can continue calling me Xoxo. I like it.'

Every day, they impatiently waited to read what Xoxo had written today. And whenever they were allowed in the kitchen, they tried to make something delicious smelling for Xoxo. Invariably, it would be a cookie with lots of chocolate and vanilla essence so that Xoxo could get a good sniff. Sometimes, they made cookies with cardamom powder, too.

Xoxo restarted his exercise of managing everyone on the dining table during dinner. The only difference was that now the children knew that Xoxo was directing them like an orchestra. It was a game with the children eating and laughing secretly, and their mother and father were happy to see the children happy.

Then, one day, Xoxo disappeared! They searched for him everywhere. The only way to find him was by looking for the small cloth fragment on his arm or when he wrote something. But he did not write anything for the last two days, nor could they see the cloth bit. In desperation, Opal took Chutney in her lap and went with him everywhere so that he would lick Xoxo whenever he was near him. Nothing yielded. Chutney enjoyed being in Opal's lap but did not lick the air.

'Let's go for a picnic again. Maybe we'll find Xoxo there.'

Shailendra and Opal perked up at this. They took permission from their mother, who readily agreed. Of late, the children have been spending too much time at home and in the kitchen. They should be playing outside much more. She packed their food and Chutney's milk too. Shailendra kept a notepad and a pen in his backpack. Xoxo would want to share his experience with them. But where was Xoxo?

'Mummy, put some chocolate biscuits and vanilla wafers also,' Opal said nonchalantly.

'Okay,' Neelam answered, though she was surprised. Opal was not particularly fond of biscuits.

They went outside in the jungle, which was not dangerous, at least, that is what the adults thought. It worked very well for the children. Along the sides of the jungle ran paddy fields, where velvety paddy grew. Their father knew a couple of farmers, so the parents had the reassurance that they would be immediately contacted in case of any emergency. These were two farmer couples who could be called genteel farmers. They were educated people who gave up their well-paying jobs to become farmers. They were committed to farming, and they liked growing things.

So Krish, Shailendra, and Opal, with Chutney, went to the jungle to look for Xoxo. They crossed the stream and went and sat under the shade of the Jungle Jalebi tree.

'Xoxo,' Opal called. No response, no fluttering of the tiny bit of cloth, nor did Chutney trot anywhere or lick the air.

'Let's cross the paddy field; maybe he's floated to that side by mistake or gone to meet somebody,' Krish suggested.

'Gone to meet somebody? Whatever do you mean Krish bhaiya? Do you think he has friends? Are they ghosts or human beings like us?' Opal was quick to ask.

'Don't know, Oppie, it could be so or not. Maybe he's hurt, we have to find out. We cannot leave him to look after himself. He's a different kind of ghost. He needs looking after.'

They nodded. 'Yes, Xoxo did need looking after, and it was their job now to take care of him.'

They walked along the paddy fields until they reached the other side. They were surprised. It looked the same as the side from which they had come. There was a Jungle Jalebi tree also. How could that be possible? How could everything be the same? They were puzzled.

Gradually, the differences began sinking in. For one, this jungle was too quiet, as if waiting for anyone to make a move so that it could jump and grab them. Their hair rose. Why? They didn't know. They looked around. The

Jungle Jalebi tree was much brighter than the tree on the other side, and its fruits were bigger and more colourful. Shailendra went near it to pluck a few fruits, but Krish bhaiya stopped him.

'No, Shailendra, don't! We will first look for Xoxo, then do anything else.'

'Uh, Okay,' I was just comparing the fruits.

They walked some more. Opal even called out, 'Xoxo, are you here? Where are you? Xoxo? Give us a sign so that we know that you are here.'

No reply, only silence. The kids kept walking. It was as if this side of the jungle was a mirror to the other side of the jungle.

'Look, there is a house there!' Shailendra said in amazement, 'Doesn't it look exactly like our own house? Let's go there.'

Suddenly, Chutney whimpered. He was on the ground; the grass was soft, so Opal had put him down. Quickly, Opal picked him up. She nuzzled his nose. Chutney gave her a lick.

'What baby? Why are you scared?' she spoke to him softly. Chutney gave a small whimper that soon turned into a happy yip. Suddenly, Chutney licked the air happily and gave a small yip again.

'Xoxo!' Xoxo was here. Immediately, Shailendra took out the notepad and pen and pointed it to where Chutney was licking the air. It was Xoxo, indeed, but a very weak Xoxo. He tried to hold the pen but could not. They could make out that it kept slipping from his hands.

'Wait!' Opal put her hands in her bag, 'Don't exert yourself, Xoxo, you'll become weaker, smell these first.'

She took some Oreos and other vanilla cream-filled biscuits and put them where Chutney was licking the air. They waited. After a few minutes, the pen rose, slanted at first, then straight, and then it began scratching on the paper. Xoxo had still not settled with his writing; he had to practice a lot.

'THERE IS A WICKED GHOST HERE. I WILL TELL YOU ABOUT IT LATER. THIS SIDE OF THE JUNGLE IS NOT SAFE. DON'T TOUCH OR EAT ANYTHING. LET US GO BACK FIRST.'

***

The Magic Unfolds

Xoxo's handwriting was full of big and small curves and spikes. The children took some time to read it. The jungle had become too quiet as if waiting to jump upon them.

Quickly, they gathered their things and started going back. Opal had Chutney in her arms. Krish and Shailendra were walking a bit behind. They were with Xoxo. Shailendra had the plate of biscuits in his hand so that Xoxo could smell them. They followed Xoxo, or the tiny cloth floating drunkenly in the air. Somehow, they found it difficult to go back. Their feet seemed tied down with rocks. It was difficult to put one foot in front of the other. They were panting by now. Somehow, they reached home, took out their shoes and went straight to their room.

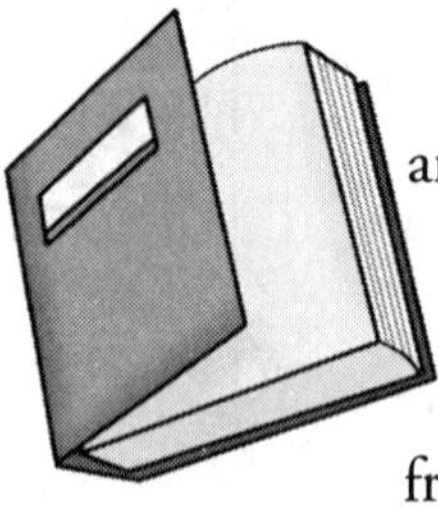

The heaviness on their feet vanished, and they felt fine again.

'What was that?' Shailendra asked. They were all confused and a bit scared. They saw Xoxo writing something frantically on the paper. He kept on writing and writing. In the meantime, Opal got some more food and kept it on the study table for Xoxo. Then they settled down, Krish with his mobile, Shailendra with Krish's iPad and Opal with her drawing and shading. She did not begin her painting because it would have become messy to clear up hurriedly. They had to read and decipher Xoxo's handwriting.

They would frequently look up to check whether Xoxo had finished or not.

'Looks as if Xoxo is writing a book,' Krish commented, though to particularly no one. They smiled.

After an hour or so, Xoxo stopped. He dropped the pen, and it clattered to the ground. They were startled. Xoxo was tired. He had written quite a lot, more than three pages. The children would have a tough time reading these pages. But they were eager to know what he had written.

'Let us all take one page each. After we finish reading, we'll put the story together. If we all read from the first page, it will take a long time.'

The others nodded. It was a practical solution. They were curious to know what Xoxo had written on these three pages. They started slowly. It was difficult to read Xoxo's handwriting. It was like a jigsaw puzzle. There were some words that they could not understand. But they plodded on. Then, they put the three pages together. What came out of those pages was scary but exciting, too. Xoxo had written that there were two more ghosts on the other side of the paddy fields, and they lived or stayed in a house which looked like theirs. Those were the evil ghosts, the cruel kind. Even the Jungle Jalebi tree was a ghost tree. It had bright and tempting fruits to lure and catch anyone who tried to pluck its fruit.

'I HAVE A MAGICAL COMPASS WHICH ALWAYS POINTS OUT WHERE WICKED GHOSTS ASSEMBLE. I HAVE FORGOTTEN WHERE I HAVE KEPT IT. I HAD IT WHEN I WAS ALIVE. MY WICKED RELATIVES KILLED ME IN THEIR GREED TO HAVE THIS HOUSE. THEN, THEY KILLED EACH OTHER IN THEIR GREED. THEY STOLE MY COMPASS, TOO, TO PROTECT THEMSELVES. THEY HAVE HIDDEN MY COMPASS ON THE OTHER SIDE OF THE PADDY FIELD. I HAD GONE THERE TO SEARCH FOR THE COMPASS TO GIVE IT TO YOU. BUT I BECAME SO WEAK THAT I COULD NOT SEARCH PROPERLY.'

'Wow!' Krish exclaimed. They were all agog with wonder and curiosity. A magic compass! Just imagine. Xoxo also wrote that the compass pointed at all the evil and gloomy things. Xoxo had written many other things which they could not read.

'We'll try later on,' Krish bhaiya declared. They were all too thrilled and excited to read any further.

'Should we go tomorrow, Xoxo?' Shailendra asked. There was no answer, nor was the bit of cloth moving. It just lay on the ground without any movement.

Opal guessed correctly, 'I think Xoxo is too tired

and weak. It may take him a day or two to recoup fully. Meanwhile, I'll go to the kitchen and cook something for Xoxo,' She kept the paper on the table and got up to go to the kitchen.

'Oppie, wait,' Shailendra too got up, 'You don't know cooking. The most which mummy has allowed you is to assemble the salad.'

Opal stopped. Well, that was a problem. But she brightened up, 'Remember, dadi had written some easy recipes for me. I am sure I can make something out of those recipes.'

Shailendra and Krish looked at each other.

'Okay then, we'll also help you. You can tell us what to do,' Krish said tactfully, knowing Opal would not like it if he said he would cook.

Opal smiled. She was relieved, too. She liked to be with her mother in the kitchen, and her mother allowed her to help with little things. Opal was fond of the idea of baking. She liked the whirring of the mixer, the way her mother carefully measured the ingredients and then mixed them one by one. She also liked to sieve the flour with the baking powder and the pinch of salt which her mother put in the cake or cookie mixture, explaining that it brought out the sweetness of the cake. Another thing which she had noticed was her mother using brown sugar in some cookies and cakes. Neelam said that brown sugar increased the taste.

But Opal was still too young to cook. She was relieved when Krish and Shailendra came to her rescue.

'Um, what shall we make? I know what we'll make!'

Opal brightened, 'We'll make chocolate chip cookies! I'll take out mummy's cooking diary.' Krish was fond of cooking. Whenever he had time, he used to go to the kitchen and cook himself some simple dishes, like mushrooms with cheese and cayenne pepper. But Opal was correct; they had to cook something that was not only delicious but smelt great, too. Xoxo's survival depended on comforting food smells. He was so weak that he could not sit with them for dinner and smell the aromas of the dishes.

Opal took out her mother's diary and opened the page of the recipe for chocolate chip cookies. Opal knew where all the baking ingredients were. She read out the recipe, and the boys measured it.

'Okay, bhaiya, I'll call out the ingredients one after another and you take them out.'

'Okay,' both of them said.

Krish and Shailendra carefully measured the

- 1 cup butter
- 1 cup white sugar
- ½ cup brown sugar
- 1 ½ tsp vanilla essence
- 2 eggs
- 2 ½ cups flour
- 1 tsp baking soda
- ½ baking powder
- ½ tsp salt
- 2 cups chocolate chips

ingredients and began mixing–the dry ingredients followed by the wet. In the end, they added the chocolate chips. Opal tasted the dough with one finger, 'Super, bhaiya, it's super tasty,' the boys tasted it, too. It was good. They then made the cookies with their hands, laid them on a baking tray, and put them in the oven. But they had forgotten to preheat the oven. The fact was that they didn't know that they had to preheat the oven. They kept peeping at it to see the progress of their biscuits. Ultimately, after forty minutes or so, they seemed done. Krish opened the hot oven door with the help of oven mitts and emptied all the cookies on a plate. They didn't know that the cookies had to be cooled down first. They each had one hot cookie, 'Oh my God, this is the tastiest cookie that I have ever had!' exclaimed Opal. The boys nodded. It was indeed very delicious. The size of the cookies was a trifle bigger than you would expect a regular cookie to be, but it did not matter to the children; they would have more to eat in one biscuit.

'What's happening?' They were startled. It was Neelam coming to check what was happening in the kitchen. She smelt the vanilla and the chocolate and guessed the children must be doing something.

'Oh, Chachi, you scared us. Come and have some cookies, fresh hot cookies, Chachi,' Krish invited his aunt inside the kitchen. The children weren't very sure about their mother's reaction. Maybe Krish bhaiya's presence would mollify her if she was angry.

'Chachi, will you have tea with the cookies? I make

nice lemon tea.'

Neelam smiled at Krish's attempt to pacify her. She didn't mind the children cooking a few allowed things provided an older person was there, in this case, Krish.

'Okay, Krish, I wouldn't mind a cup of tea,' she bit into a biscuit, 'Mmm! It's delicious! Where did you all learn to make it?'

The children heaved a sigh of relief. Krish quickly boiled water, added a sachet of green tea and a few drops of lemon and brought it to his aunt. He placed the sugar pot beside the cup on the tray. 'What a well-mannered boy,' Neelam thought, 'Shailendra and Opal will be in good hands in these holidays.' She stayed with the children for some time, then went out on the veranda to continue with her new painting.

'Make sure you clean up before you leave the kitchen,' she gave a parting shot.

'Yes, ma'am,' three voices chorused.

Shailendra kept the biscuits in a tin, Opal put three biscuits on a plate, and Krish wiped the platform with the kitchen cloth. After this, they ran upstairs to Shailendra's bedroom with the biscuit plate. Xoxo was lying under the study table, still weak, though they could now see some movement. Opal put the plate of biscuits beside Xoxo and gave Chutney his milk in a small bowl. Chutney was now trying to drink milk from a bowl, though he messed up quite a lot.

There was a sharp improvement in Xoxo's body.

'Oh! What delicious smells!' he wanted to ask the

children whether they had made the biscuits themselves, but that required him to get up and write on the study table. 'Later,' he thought, 'later, when I have enough strength. But first, I must become strong and tell them about the evil and wicked ghost on the other side of the paddy fields.'

Xoxo took deep breaths to smell as much of the vanilla and chocolate biscuits as he could. Then, after ten minutes or so, he felt strong enough to stand up. He was near the study table. He took the pen and wrote, 'I want a new sheet.'

Shailendra read what he had written, 'Yes sir, Xoxo sir, a new sheet coming up.'

Xoxo smiled. Of course, nobody could see him smiling, but they could feel his smile.

There were so many crucial things that Xoxo wanted to tell the children. One was to find a compass, which would point at the exact location of the ghosts staying, either in the opposite house or in the huge Jungle Jalebi tree. The second thing was a mirror hidden near the paddy fields. This mirror could duplicate anything but in the wrong way. It was such a dangerous mirror that if it fell into the wrong hands, it will replicate every evil thing or creature. And the world would be destroyed in a matter of days or weeks. He had to make the children understand the gravity of the situation. The third important thing was to find the will he had made before his death.

Being a loner when he was alive, he did not have many friends or people to talk with. His wife had died, and his only daughter had broken off her relationship with him to live abroad with her husband. Xoxo had no contact with her. Though he did have some money, and of course, this house and another in a different part of the town, it was his house that he was worried about. 'But I will write about that later on,' he thought. 'The children will be confused if I tell them so many things at once.'

So, Xoxo thought hard. He had to choose the most significant action first. He had to write slowly and simply for the children to understand him and not get scared. He decided that he will explain about the magic mirror first. That was the first thing they had to find and break so that it did not multiply bad things anymore. He began writing. Too bad he could neither be heard nor seen. He began writing.

'THERE IS A MIRROR WITH THOSE WICKED GHOSTS ON THE OTHER SIDE OF THE PADDY FIELD. EARLIER, THERE WAS JUST A SMALL JUNGLE AND HILLS AND MOUNTAINS AFTER THAT. IT WAS NOT DANGEROUS AT ALL. THEN, THE TWO WICKED GHOSTS CAME HERE AND SOMEHOW DISCOVERED THE MAGICAL MIRROR WHICH MULTIPLIES EVERYTHING. THAT IS HOW THEY CREATED THE OTHER PART OF THE JUNGLE, EXACTLY LIKE THIS PART. VERY SOON, THEY WILL REPLICATE MANY BAD THINGS, TOO. THEY MAY POINT TO THE MIRROR AND MULTIPLY WILD ANIMALS OR OTHER WICKED GHOSTS. THESE THINGS WILL DESTROY GOODNESS ON EARTH. WE HAVE TO FIND OR STEAL THE MIRROR AND BREAK OR HIDE IT. NO MATTER WHAT WE DO, WE HAVE TO DO IT QUICKLY, BEFORE ANY REAL DAMAGE.'

Xoxo was tired, very tired. He had written so much after such a long time. The pen fell from his hands, and even he lay down. Chutney came, curled up beside him and went to sleep as if it was the most normal thing to do. Opal looked up. Quickly, she kept the plate of biscuits near his face so that he could easily smell them and get up. But Xoxo was now really tired. His experiences of the past few days had drained his energy. He had also not slept adequately ever since his death. He was just not comfortable with his new life or rather a new way of living, whatever kind it was, ever since he became a ghost. He did not know why his or the souls of some other people did not pass over after their deaths. Maybe it had to do with some work which only they could do on this Earth. It was now in the company of these children who understood him that Xoxo found himself relaxing a little. On top of that was the unconditional love from the pup Chutney that made him feel wanted and loved and which gave back some of his self-respect. It was mainly Chutney's love that made him feel wanted and loved again.

***

Mirror, Mirror on the Wall

When Xoxo did not get up for some time, Opal correctly assumed that Xoxo was relaxing after the torture of the last two or three days. The boys were busy with their gadgets. She quickly got up and picked up the page to read what he had written. She was startled when she read it. She read it again to make sure that she understood what was written.

'Shailendra bhaiya, Krish bhaiya, come and read what Xoxo has written!' both jumped and came to her. They also read, unbelievingly, what Xoxo had written.

'Oh!' Shailendra could only utter this.

'Oh, My God!' exclaimed Krish, 'Xoxo!' he looked around for Xoxo till he espied the tell-tale piece of cloth. But Xoxo was not getting up. He was sleeping peacefully after years.

'I think he's exhausted,' piped in Opal, 'We should let him rest. I think he will get up at dinner time when he gets the smell of food.'

Having no other solution, the boys had to agree. All three of them sat together and tried to think of ways of searching for the evil magic mirror.

'We will first have to ask Xoxo about the size and shape of the mirror, whether it is a small hand mirror or a large one like people have in their dressers. We will have to search for it methodically, you know, bit by bit. If only Xoxo could talk, it would have been easier to find the evil mirror,' Krish expressed himself. The others agreed.

Opal shared her thoughts, 'Krish bhaiya, we had seen Xoxo once when he had tried to run through the wall in the living room. I think if he has more energy, he might be able to say a few words.'

'Yes, bhaiya,' Shailendra agreed, 'We did see Xoxo. He was like a huge bedsheet hung on a long bamboo stick.'

'I think if we give many different good-smelling things to Xoxo, he might get more strength. We might be able to see his form, and who knows, maybe he would be able to speak.'

Krish agreed, 'We'll have to hurry with such things. We have to find the evil mirror before those wicked ghosts multiply the things they need to rule over this world.'

'Krish bhaiya, we will have to find good-smelling things for Xoxo. Writing down everything is a very long and tiring process for Xoxo,' Shailendra suggested, 'We have one great emergency, that of searching for the mirror and destroying it. Without Xoxo quickly directing us, we are unable to do anything.'

He looked around for Opal, but she was not there. Surprised, he called out for her.

'Coming,' Opal answered from below. Soon, she was there with them, carrying a large basket. Before they could ask, she answered them herself, 'I went to mummy's bedroom, and I went to the kitchen and the storeroom, too. Mummy has a whole lot of things in her dresser. I got a small perfume, which I know mummy will not miss much. I also got a few other things from mummy's room, like a few oils she uses for her headaches and massages. I like the smell of spirit, so I got that too,' Opal took out some other aromatic bottles from the bag and showed it to them.

'Good girl, Oppie,' Shailendra patted her on the head. Opal smiled.

'We will put these bottles one by one near Xoxo and see his reaction; if he likes a smell, we'll keep that near him,' saying this, he kept the small bottle of perfume which Opal had brought. First, he opened the cap and sprayed some perfume near Xoxo. After a few seconds, the finger with the cloth moved a bit, and it seemed that Xoxo was sitting up. That was it. No other change. They kept changing the bottles one by one and keeping them beside Xoxo for one or two minutes. They were unsure, but it seemed he had come to his senses and was thoroughly enjoying the process. He would either move his finger when he liked a smell or not move it when he did not like it.

It was then that they noticed a shimmery shadow of Xoxo. It came and it went.

Opal almost screamed, 'Look, I just saw him! Did you see him? I think he liked one of the smells.'

'Or maybe more than one,' Krish was excited, too. To see a ghost by making him inhale the scent he liked, and which made him take form, was one of the most exciting things in their lives. If Krish could thank God for all the adventures he would definitely have done so. There was so much of adventure and excitement waiting for them. On the other hand, Xoxo was trying to segregate the different kinds of smells. He recalled some scents, too. Some of the scents revived his long-lost memories. He did not like the perfume which was of Opal's mother. It was good but too feminine. But there was one smell he particularly liked and had used when he was alive. Even now, it almost brought him back to life. By almost it meant that his form developed somehow, even for half a minute only. But by the time he looked around for the smell, the children had removed it and were now trying another one.

Gradually, through many hits and misses, the children concluded that the one smell Xoxo liked was the smell of tea tree oil that their mother used for her headaches and other such problems. Krish smelled it. It was very sharp and pungent, almost reaching the apex of the head through the nose. Another smell which Xoxo liked was the smell of varnish and paints. Xoxo was an artist of sorts when he was alive. He loved to paint in his free time. The smell of paint and varnish reminded of happy and satisfying times. He had started shimmering after smelling these smells. Once the children understood that Xoxo liked these smells, they kept these bottles near him in the hope that they would be able to see Xoxo and maybe, after some practice, he would talk to them too. Then, it would become much easier to find the evil mirror.

'I think, at best, we should give Xoxo about two days to show himself to us. Then, we can wait for another two days for him to speak. We don't have time. I hope he starts speaking,' Krish spoke fervently.

'He will, Krish bhaiya,' then turning towards Xoxo, Shailendra asked, 'What do you say, Xoxo? Are four days enough for you to show yourself and start speaking?'

Xoxo laughed out loud, 'I can now itself,' he said loudly. But the children didn't hear. Opal suspected something. It was as if the wind was churning in slow motion where Xoxo was sitting.

'Xoxo, are you saying something?' she asked. The air moved some more. Xoxo was trying to talk.

'Here, smell some more of this tea tree oil. Maybe it will clear your vocal cords too,' Opal put the small bottle of tea tree oil under his nose. Xoxo took a deep breath and lo and behold! There he was! They could now fully see him. He was a tall, lanky man, though wavy. He was not visible clearly. It was as if they could see a wavy outline, which disappeared soon after.

'Okay,' Krish took a decision, 'This will be all for a couple of hours. It has been an exciting time for us, but it must be very tiring and confusing for Xoxo. We must now let him be.'

Shailendra agreed, and so did Opal. 'Yes, bhaiya, he must be so tired, confused and anxious. It seems as if he has all the worries of the world on his shoulders.'

Xoxo heard the children. Though he did not want to rest, he knew the children were right. The past few hours had been strange and hectic for him. Earlier, he was just a helpless spectator. He could see and not do anything about it. For some reason, which he could not think of, he could not leave this world and enter another realm, higher or lower. But now things were changing so fast. From an insignificant ghost to a 'going to become a powerful ghost' was beyond Xoxo's imagination. He had started getting a form, and, very soon, he might be able to speak too. This was too startling and exciting for him. But it was too strenuous also.

There were so many emotions going on inside his head and heart. He was grateful that the children had given him a new lease of life. Well, he was technically dead, so the children had given him a new lease of hope. He knew about the evil mirror, but the thought had never entered his mind to do something about it. Whenever he went to the other side of the fields, his brother ghosts would offer him food in the form of blood and flesh of animals. But Xoxo could never eat that. He gagged on them. His so-called friends would then beat him into a pulp. Later on, Xoxo became a punching bag for them. Earlier, they used to beat him on an excuse, but lately, they had begun torturing him without any reason. It had become hell for him. Just the thought of going there gave him the shivers. But it was mandatory for the ghosts who had to stay back here on this Earth to mark their attendance in *The Ghosts Book of Earthly Creatures*. Failing to comply with this condition would ban their souls forever from leaving the Earth. It did help, however, when you helped people of this world and prevented violence. When Xoxo felt part of his strength revived, other thoughts came to his mind. He would think how he could save most of the world by destroying the evil mirror which multiplied things. He knew this was possible only with the help of the children.

Initially, only Opal understood how he could get some energy. Later, the boys, too, caught on and even made the aromatic chocolate cookies for him. Opal got so many different kinds of smells for him. The children gave him his strength and his self-respect back. And now they were in danger because of his ghost brethren. He decided to do everything in his power to save the children from the evil magic mirror. But he must rest first. It was the beginning of his revival. He may not get another chance to help the world. Xoxo felt as if the whole world depended on him. He had to do things carefully and quickly. The most practical thing was to rest so that he could think and act clearly. Now, Xoxo knew he had to do something before passing on to the great unknown.

His creator would give him his body through these children because he had this burning desire to set things right. He knew that the body he would regain would be just a temporary thing. He would go back to being an invisible and mute ghost. It was his last chance to go to the next world. So, Xoxo went to one of the beds and lay there upside down because that is how the good ghosts rested.

***

Tik, Tik, Tik

The next day, they went to search for the evil mirror. They were all rested and very excited. Both the boys helped Opal pack the essentials–food, water, towels etc. Krish took his multitool pocket kit, too. Shailendra took his torch, compass, and a small knife just in case.

By nine, they were ready to go. Neelam had packed a delicious picnic hamper for them. Neelam and her husband Hemant were happy that the children were enjoying their holidays. The mountains and the jungle behind their house, too, helped in their spirit of adventure. It was good that the children were getting along with each other. Neelam had doubts whether Shailendra and Opal would get along with Krish, but either Krish came down to their level or Shailendra and Opal grew up to his level. The fact was that all three got along like a house on fire. Chutney, the pup, was another factor which bonded them, Neelam thought affectionately. If Neelam had even the slightest idea of where their real bonding came from, all hell would have broken loose.

Neelam and her husband approved of the children going for hikes in the jungle. It was a safe jungle, not very large like a forest, just a place left barren. But it grew up beautifully like an enchanted garden. It had flowering shrubs, friendly trees with strong branches that could be easily climbed, and no dangerous animals around. The paddy fields meant there would always be people around. After the paddy fields lived their friends, the Vermas, Lalit and Aarti, who had their farmhouse there. Neelam knew the children would be looked after in case of a mishap. Sometimes, adults shouldn't know much about their children's activities.

They were now in the thick part of the jungle.

'Now what, Xoxo?' Opal asked, 'Where do we begin our search from?'

Xoxo could not speak. He had smelt the sumptuous breakfast that Neelam had made. That had given him enough strength for more than two days. Opal had thoughtfully packed all the smell bottles that Xoxo had loved last night, especially the tea tree oil bottle. After Xoxo inhaled large amounts of the tea tree liquid, he took some form, though only for a few minutes. Opal was sure that if Xoxo was given the right smells, he would take form and become visible in a couple of days. But they did not have much time at present. It was most important to find the evil mirror. They followed Xoxo's finger with the strip of cloth wrapped around it. That was their GPS. Xoxo was charged up and raring to go. He had a rough idea of where the magic mirror was. So he just floated over the paddy field to reach the other side. The paddy had been planted some time ago, and now these fields were a lush neon green. The fields were covered with water. The children could not wade over the water and cross to the other side. That would have spoilt their clothes and crushed the paddy.

'Wait, Xoxo! We will come slowly. We have to walk across the paddy fields and then follow you,' Shailendra called out in panic. But Xoxo did not hear him. He was so full of his newfound strength that he just sailed through the paddy fields. Krish, Shailendra and Opal tried to walk as fast as they could on the mud tracks but were not as quick as Xoxo. On the other hand, Xoxo looked back after reaching the other side. The trio wasn't there. 'Oh! Where were they? Did they go back? Oh no! That would be a disaster.' Xoxo looked around and tried calling them. He called them by their names but got no response. Then he remembered. He did not have a voice as yet. Forget voice, he did not even have a solid form. He was like the wind, sometimes a bit noisy but invisible. Like the wind, Xoxo could only be felt. Dejected, he stood on the periphery of the last paddy field, not knowing what to do. He fearfully looked around. His other ghost kin stayed somewhere here itself. If somehow they discovered him here, they would torture him again and beat him if he did not eat or drink their kind of food. Because he was much weaker than them, he always lost to them. They were so strong that they could change into whatever form they wanted to. Xoxo was sure that the wicked ghosts had made these houses on this side of the paddy fields with the help of the magic mirror. He was too scared to stay here for long. But without the children's help, he wouldn't be able to fight his ghost enemies. Xoxo sat down. He looked around for the children. He looked at the paddy fields. They were not there. He had told them to follow him. Had they got scared? He doubted it.

'There you are, Xoxo!' Krish cried out, 'You just floated to this side. We did not want to cross the paddy fields. That would have damaged the paddy plants, and we would have become dirty; I hope you didn't worry much.'

Xoxo stood up. Now that he had seen the children, his anxiety and fear turned into anger. He straightened up, **'WHAT! I WORRY? DON'T BE RIDICULOUS. THERE IS NOTHING TO WORRY ABOUT!'** Xoxo almost danced away his tension, **'I WOULD HAVE FINISHED OFF THESE GHOSTS JUST LIKE THAT, POUF! EVEN WITHOUT THE EVIL MIRROR!'**

The children neither saw Xoxo dancing nor could they hear him. They only saw a piece of cloth fluttering in the air, a little more than usual. Chutney gave a yip and licked Xoxo to soothe him. Xoxo hugged Chutney, who hugged him back. The temporary anxiety was over. Now for some real work!

'FOLLOW ME,' roared Xoxo. They all followed him happily. Not that they could hear him, but they found the air around them was filled with excitement and hope. Chutney, too, was trotting beside them. He liked walking now. Opal picked him up whenever she thought he was tired or could not catch up with their walking.

Xoxo took them to the place where there was more vegetation.

'So strange, this place is exactly like our side. See, even the stream and the Jungle Jalebi tree are here,' Krish looked around, 'How can this be possible?' he asked Xoxo, or the fragment of cloth floating around them.

Xoxo cleared his throat and began answering them. But, of course, they could not hear him. Opal was sure that Xoxo was saying something. She could make out by the movement of the small cloth; it was as if Xoxo was pointing a finger here, there, and so many other places. Xoxo was answering Krish.

'THIS ENTIRE PLACE, THE MIRROR COPY OF YOUR SIDE OF THE PLACE, HAS NOT BEEN MADE BY PEOPLE LIKE YOU. HAVE YOU NOTICED ANY DIFFERENCE?' he demanded. Not getting an answer, Xoxo continued, 'THAT IS BECAUSE THE EVIL MIRROR HAS MADE ALL THIS. IT IS JUST A BIT BRIGHTER THAN YOUR SIDE OF THE PLACE. THIS IS BECAUSE THE MIRROR COPIES ONLY WHAT IS REFLECTED IN IT. IT'S LIKE A CAMERA WHICH NEEDS PROPER LIGHTING TO MAKE GOOD PICTURES. THE OTHERS MUST HAVE POINTED TO THE MIRROR WHEN THERE MUST HAVE BEEN TOO MUCH LIGHT. THAT IS WHY THE PICTURE ON THIS SIDE IS BRIGHTER THAN THE REAL PLACE ON YOUR SIDE. BUT THE SIMILARITY ENDS HERE. IT IS JUST A BEAUTIFUL PLACE. EVERYTHING ELSE HERE IS DARK, BLACK AND EVIL. THE FRUITS OF THE

JUNGLE JALEBI ARE FULL OF WORMS, AND THE BEAUTIFUL STREAM ON THIS SIDE IS FULL OF POISONOUS SNAKES AND SHARP, DEADLY ROCKS. THOUGH ITS WATERS LOOK CALM, THE FLOW IS SO STRONG THAT IT WILL EITHER CARRY YOU DEEP INSIDE AND BURY YOU OR BEAT YOU AGAINST ITS ROCKS INTO PIECES,' Xoxo would have continued but he paused when he realised that his words flew away with the wind. The children could not hear him. 'I must do something about it,' Xoxo thought fiercely. 'I have to guide the children correctly so that they can find the evil mirror and destroy it.' 'But how do I do it? I have to have enough strength to speak so that the children can hear and understand me.' Xoxo was also scared that the children would either drink the water of the stream or even eat the fruit of the Jungle Jalebi. That would be disastrous. The only way was to inhale as much of the smells collected by Opal as possible.

The rest of the day, Xoxo guided them as well as he could to search for the mirror. Once in a while, even he got confused whether they were in a real place or an image made by the mirror. If he could find the magic compass, that would have helped them greatly. But the children may get confused, he thought. First, search for the magic compass, then the evil, magic mirror. There was no time for so many things. They had to stay away from the wicked ghosts, too. If they discovered Xoxo in their area, they would again capture him and torture him just for fun. He could not even imagine what they would do to the children.

By evening, they were all tired, Opal more so, as she had to look after Chutney too.

'We should go back now,' Krish declared. He was the eldest, and he rightly felt that he had to look after his younger siblings. Somehow, he felt that even Xoxo was confused, or maybe they couldn't follow him. They had to go back and decide on a new strategy. He repeated his words loudly this time so that Xoxo could also hear him. They went back.

'Oh, you've come back right on time. I knew you all would be hungry, so I've made these yummy *Shimla mirch* and paneer toasted sandwiches for all of you. Go clean up and come down fast,' Neelam said happily.

'Yay!' exclaimed Shailendra, and they all ran happily upstairs. All except for Xoxo. Xoxo, too, was quite tired after the whole day of searching for the evil mirror. Everyone, including him, was so excited that he didn't get much chance to sniff the chocolate biscuits and the other smells that Opal had so carefully packed. When he returned home with the children, he immediately perked at the piquant and savoury smell of the capsicum and paneer fried in butter with just a hint of *Kashmiri mirch*.

The aroma of the toasted sandwiches filled the kitchen and its surroundings. Xoxo was hooked to its smell. He sat on the dining chair at the far end, closed his eyes and noisily inhaled the aroma. Not that Neelam heard it. Xoxo had made this chair his own. Nobody sat here. Sometimes, Hemant put a book or a paper here, but Xoxo did not mind. He just sat atop the book/newspaper, and nobody noticed anything.

The children rushed down. Opal had noticed that Xoxo had not gone upstairs with them.

'You go and eat Opal; I'll give milk to Chutney and

come,' Krish said. He knew that Opal was tired and hungry. Afterwards, he sat on the dining table and stuffed his plate with the sandwiches.

'Mmm! Chachi, these sandwiches are delicious!' Neelam smiled and passed him a cup of milk.

Opal sat on the opposite side and quietly gestured to the empty chair on the far end. They looked. Sure enough, they saw a piece of cloth fluttering there. So Xoxo was sitting there from the beginning. He must have got his energy back. But this was not working out. They would have to think of a way to make Xoxo talk.

The next day, they sat in the garden on the pretext of completing their projects for the school. Thoughtfully, they also placed a chair, a notepad and a pen for Xoxo. Chutney, too, was there, trotting here and there on the green lawn and trying to bark. Opal and Shailendra had already chosen Krish as their leader. Krish himself took on the mantle of leading towards a good solution. The problem was so huge. They could not do anything without him, the same way that Xoxo could not do without them. Krish turned to Xoxo, 'Xoxo, we have given you much strength by giving you many kinds of smells. But we cannot really follow you in the jungle because we can't see or hear you. Can you suggest anything we can do so that you get more strength and we can see and hear you?'

Xoxo was fresh now. Last night's snacks and dinner had given him enough strength to pick up the pen and write. Xoxo began writing. His writing was slow and laborious. The children waited.

After a wait of ten minutes or so, Xoxo put his pen down. They peered eagerly at the paper. Xoxo had written more than half a page. But it was so disappointing. Probably, Xoxo was excited or had more energy this morning, every word was joined. As a result, it looked as if a long line of big, drunken ants had walked over the page. They could not read it! What should they do now?

'Xoxo, can you write more and separate one word from the other? It's so important that we hear and see you. We have to find the evil mirror as soon as possible,' Shailendra tried to coax Xoxo. For a minute, there was no response. Then, as if in slow motion, Xoxo picked up the pen and wrote one word repeatedly. It was **'PEACOCK, PEACOCK, PEACOCK'**

'Peacock?' Krish mused, 'Does he mean a real live peacock or a peacock feather?'

'Krish bhaiya,' Opal piped in, 'Mummy has a fan made of peacock feathers that she had bought at a fair. She doesn't use it. It's on one of the shelves. I'll run and get it. Maybe Xoxo is asking for that.'

Both Krish and Shailendra nodded. Opal ran inside and was back in a jiffy. She held a fan made of peacock feathers. She gave it to Krish. Krish shook it to get rid of any dust, then slowly, he swayed it all over Xoxo's body or at least where he thought Xoxo's body would be. In the meantime, Opal and Shailendra waved the biscuit and the tea tree oil

near his nose. Neelam, their mother, looked out of the window from the living room. She saw Krish slowly moving her peacock fan in the air, and it looked as if Opal and Shailendra were slowly swaying with the fan holding a few things in their hands.

'They must be doing some make-believe acting. Maybe it's a part of their project,' she smiled and continued with her work. Had she watched them for some more time, her mind would have been blown away with the picture in front of her. But Neelam got busy with her work.

Meanwhile, the children's mouths almost fell with shock and fright. For, right in front of them, a figure was evolving. It wasn't exactly a human figure; it was more like a slim tent over a pole. However, it was not very surprising as Opal and Shailendra have had a glimpse of Xoxo. It was good that they could see him now. But they really wanted to hear him so that he could direct him to the evil mirror that duplicated mainly evil things.

'Xoxo, can you talk?' Krish asked him doubtfully.

The tent turned towards him, **'YES, I CAN,'** they heard a dull, heavy voice as if the sound were coming out in slow motion. But they definitely knew that it was Xoxo. They were so happy that they held hands and danced around the long pole-like Xoxo. Opal was so excited that she sang a poem in which she remembered only two lines, but it was enough to show her happiness and relief. These lines were, '*Chal mere* Xoxo, *tik tik tik. Pankh hila ke tik tik tik.*' ('Come on my Xoxo start walking *tik tik tik,* moving the feather *tik tik tik.*)

The original poem was
'Chal mere ghode tik tik tik,(Come my horse start walking tik tik tik)
Dum hila ke tik tik tik.' (move your tail tik tik tik.)

Opal improvised it. The boys found it so cute that they, too, began clapping and repeating it happily. Xoxo looked at them strangely and wondered why they were running around him and chanting something. A long-lost memory stirred in his heart and then he remembered something. The children had replaced the word *ghode* (horse) with his name Xoxo. Presently, he had accepted his name as Xoxo, but he was going to change it after the crisis of the evil mirror was over. Xoxo liked the one-line chant so much that he, too, clapped his hands and joined in. If Neelam had peered from the window, she would have seen the children happily dancing around a pole. Slowly, Xoxo faded away, and even his raspy voice stopped. There was silence.

The children waited, but there was silence. Chutney came to the fore. Till now, even he was yipping and trotting around with them. But when they stopped, he didn't want to stop. When the children didn't listen to him, he trotted towards Xoxo and began licking him in the hope that he would at least get up and join him in the jig again. They heaved a sigh of relief when the cloth on Xoxo's finger began moving feebly.

'Bhaiya,' Shailendra thought loudly, 'He must have been a ghost for a long time. He doesn't eat or drink like evil ghosts. The smells gave him energy, and the peacock feathers gave him shape and sound. It must have been too much for him. I think it will take him some time to adjust to his newfound skills.'

'You're right, Shailendra,' Krish answered, 'But we cannot give him too much time. You never know what chaos the wicked ghosts will create with the evil magic mirror.'

Opal, the problem solver, quipped in, 'Yes, bhaiya, we can take turns giving Xoxo his good smells and brush him with the peacock fan. We will divide our time into three parts. If some time is left, then Chutney will take care of it by snuggling to Xoxo.'

'Good idea, Oppie,' Shailendra mussed her hair. Opal smiled, 'I'll take the first turn, then Shailendra bhaiya and then Krish bhaiya can take his turn.'

They nodded. Xoxo was also listening. He did not have the strength to participate in the conversation. But with such eager, helpful children around him, he knew he would regain his strength quickly. Xoxo vowed to himself that he would work hard to regain his strength.

A rigorous exercise routine began between all four of them. And, of course, Chutney too. That made five of them. From seven in the morning till ten at night, they made sure that any one of them was softly brushing Xoxo with the peacock feather fan and a supply of good aromatic food was kept near him. It included tea tree oil, a little varnish, and some nail polish. Xoxo liked to smell these things. After some time, they discovered that Xoxo also liked to hear classical Hindi music. It wasn't difficult for Krish to find these songs on his iPad. They were all set now. But apart from brushing

Xoxo's body with the Peacock feather fan, the other things had to be given to Xoxo one after another, or else it led to confusion and did not have much effect on Xoxo.

So, the exercise continued, and after a couple of days, it began giving results. Xoxo started taking form from the first day itself. He already had a form, but now they could see it. They did not see him as a man's body. He again looked as if somebody had covered an off-white bedsheet over a six-foot pole. They could not see his hands or legs, and Xoxo did not walk. He glided a foot above the ground. Opal thought she saw two large eyes, but when she looked closely, they disappeared. So far, so good. Once, Xoxo picked up a pen to write something, but Shailendra stopped him.

'Xoxo, wait!' Shailendra exclaimed, 'Don't start writing! You will end up losing lots of energy. You have to preserve your energy to speak and tell us about the evil magic mirror.'

Xoxo paused as if he was thinking. Yes, what the young boy Cylinder was saying was right. He must gather all his energies. God knows what those wicked ghosts were duplicating with the mirror! He stopped and waited.

On the third day, just after breakfast, two good things happened. They had finished their breakfast and came after informing their mother that they would pack their hampers and go out into the jungle to play. Once upstairs, they began putting the essential things in one bag. It was while they were packing that they heard two unexpected sounds. The first sound was the bark of Chutney. His yip had changed into a bark, though it still sounded babyish.

Chutney himself was so excited by his own bark that he jumped around on his short, chubby legs and showed off his bark to everybody.

'Ooh! Chutney!' Opal cooed and picked him up in his arms to kiss him. Chutney licked her and then struggled out of her arms, ran to the boys, and barked and wagged his tail. Both the boys patted Chutney on the head. Chutney then went towards the pole-covered tent and barked there too.

'GOOD BOY, CHUTNEY,' and a hand came out from the pole and patted Chutney on the head.

Opal put her hands over her mouth and uttered, 'Wow!'

Shailendra and Krish too said, 'Wow!'

Xoxo himself was dazed. So many things were happening to him! It was almost like he was alive. Well, he was not going to think about that now. He had to solve the immediate crisis of the evil mirror. If only his voice would last for a few hours at least. He patted Chutney again and was surprised to see that he could still see himself. As far as Chutney was concerned, he never saw him as a ghost. For Chutney, Xoxo was as alive as any human being. Being a dog, Chutney knew from his heart who was a good person and who was not.

'LET'S NOT WASTE ANY MORE TIME. WE HAVE TO FIND THE EVIL MAGIC MIRROR BEFORE THOSE DEVILS DO ANY MORE DAMAGE.'

***

The Hunt Begins

The children stared wide-eyed and unbelievingly at Xoxo. It was almost fifteen minutes, and Xoxo's voice was still loud and strong. They woke up from their reverie, shook their heads and got up to go outside. All this time Opal was unconsciously brushing Xoxo with the peacock feather fan. That also could be a reason for Xoxo to continue talking.

Quickly, they went out. Once they reached the jungle, they turned to Xoxo.

'Where do we begin our search, Xoxo? Any idea how large the evil mirror is, and can the wicked ghosts hide it?'

'ITS SIZE IS NOT VERY LARGE. IT IS ABOUT EIGHT INCHES IN LENGTH AND BREADTH. IT HAS A HANDLE AND A FRAME. IT MULTIPLIES ONLY THE THINGS REFLECTED IN IT. THE WICKED GHOSTS ARE CLEVER

AND CUNNING. THEY MULTIPLY BAD PEOPLE AND THINGS ONLY WHEN NOBODY IS LOOKING, AND THEY ARE CUNNING ENOUGH TO HIDE IT. IN THE BEGINNING, I KNEW WHERE THEY KEPT IT, BUT NOW THEY KEEP CHANGING THE HIDING PLACES. WE WILL HAVE TO MAKE A FRESH SEARCH OR SEARCHES. ALL OF YOU, BE ON THE LOOKOUT FOR ANY DIFFERENT SHAPES OR SCENERY. SOMETIMES, THE MIRROR DOESN'T CATCH THE IMAGES PROPERLY. YOU WILL HAVE TO SEARCH FOR ANYTHING WHICH DOES NOT LOOK RIGHT.'

'That is quite a tall order, Xoxo. In the jungle, almost everything looks lopsided,' Krish remarked.

Shailendra was gung-ho about the whole thing. So was Opal. It was so much of an adventure! To prevent the wicked ghosts from duplicating evil things was so exciting. It was the best holiday. They were thrilled. First, there was a friendly ghost in their house, and then Krish bhaiya came. They adored Krish bhaiya. On top of it, Chutney came with Krish bhaiya. The adventure of a lifetime had begun. The quest for the magical evil mirror had begun.

'WE WILL BEGIN OUR SEARCH WITH THE FEW HOUSES ON THE OTHER SIDE OF THE PADDY FIELDS. THEY USED TO HIDE THE MIRROR IN ONE OF THE ABANDONED HOUSES. BUT THEY ARE VERY CUNNING; THEY KEEP CHANGING THEIR HIDING PLACE. WE SEARCH IN ONE PLACE. THEN WE GO TO OTHER PLACES TO SEARCH. IN THE MEANTIME, THESE EVIL GHOSTS WILL HIDE IT AGAIN IN THE FIRST PLACE THAT WE WOULD HAVE ALREADY SEARCHED.'

'But we are human beings, and we are more intelligent than them, and even you have the goodness of human beings. There is no doubt that we will outsmart them,' Krish answered gravely, 'It might take some time though.'

'That is what we don't have, Krish bhaiya,' Shailendra commented, 'We have to find and destroy the evil magic mirror before they change the world.'

Opal nodded, and Chutney barked in agreement. There were seven tiny houses which were not in good shape and where nobody lived. They probably were used by the labourers who came on and off to work on the farms. They used to live in these cottages or houses while they were here for work and then left after it was over.

'Let us begin from the middle house,' Opal suggested, 'and search in a zig-zag way so that the evil ghosts are unable to guess where we would search next.'

'GOOD IDEA,' Xoxo approved, **'WE WILL BEGIN WITH THE FOURTH HOUSE, THEN GO TO THE LAST HOUSE. AFTER THAT, I WILL TELL YOU WHICH HOUSE TO SEARCH NEXT. BE VERY CAREFUL, AND SEARCH IN EVERY NOOK AND CORNER OF THE HOUSE, EVEN THE SMALLEST OR THE BIGGEST PLACES, ESPECIALLY WHERE WE THINK WE WON'T FIND THE MIRROR,'** Xoxo directed them.

They went to the fourth house. It was more like a cottage. It just had one room and was covered with dust and cobwebs. A few beddings had been rolled and kept in a corner. There were some straw mats, a few kitchen utensils, a small drum for water, and a few other knick knacks left around carelessly. It was a simple house of a peasant, but there were plenty of places to hide a mirror. It was a good place to train Chutney, but they could not show him the mirror as they had not seen it as yet. They searched for the mirror everywhere but could not find it. Sometimes, Chutney distracted them when he barked at the wrong things. They were not very disappointed as this was the first house. There were six more houses and the rest of the jungle too. They searched in two more houses, without any luck.

Then strange things began happening when they entered the fourth house. First, instead of barking Chutney began yipping again as if he was scared. Then he wouldn't go inside. They had not used a leash on him yet, so Opal picked him up. They went inside. It was the same scenario as the other cottages.

'Let us fan out and search in different directions,' Krish ordered them. They nodded and went into different parts of the cottage. Chutney was scared, though this cottage was the same as others, dusty and dirty. Maybe Chutney had developed an allergy to the dust. Or it could be anything, but Opal had no time to fuss around Chutney. She kissed him and kept him in her arms while she searched for the mirror. It was tedious work, but the children and Xoxo were charged up and they searched the place with the same enthusiasm as the earlier cottages. Chutney struggled to get down from Opal's arms. By now, they knew where to search since all the cottages were the same.

Shailendra called out, 'See Xoxo, I've found this thick red cloth. Maybe they used to wrap the mirror in this.'

'Arre,' Krish said in surprise, 'Even I've found a red cloth exactly like this,' he too waved a thick red cloth.

'Bhaiya,' Opal almost whispered, 'I have also seen the same red cloth. It's lying there,' she pointed in the direction where she had seen the red cloth. They turned to look. Sure enough, there was a red cloth lying carelessly on a broken cane chair. They turned towards Xoxo, who was fading and brightening periodically. Chutney had wriggled out of Opal's arms and was now yipping and barking at the red cloth lying on the broken cane chair. His small tail was straight up, and it was not wagging. Opal went to him and tried to pick him up. The moment she touched him, he yipped and jumped three feet in the air as if a cruel enemy had attacked him. He calmed down when he saw Opal and readily came into her arms.

'THIS MEANS THAT THESE EVIL GHOSTS HAD TILL NOW KEPT THE MIRROR IN THESE RED CLOTHS. THEY MUST BE MULTIPLYING THESE PIECES OF RED CLOTHS AND THEN WRAPPING THE MIRROR IN THE CLOTH. CHUTNEY BARKING AT THE CLOTH MEANS THAT THERE IS STILL THE SMELL OF THESE GHOSTS IN THAT CLOTH. I THINK THEY HAVE JUST REMOVED THE MIRROR AND HIDDEN IT SOMEWHERE ELSE. THESE GHOSTS ARE CUNNING BUT INTELLIGENT. THEY MIGHT NOT WRAP THE EVIL MIRROR IN A RED CLOTH NOW.'

'Yes, we will continue with our search. Now we know that the evil mirror does exist, and it was here sometime back,' Krish said. They continued, but there was no trace of the evil magic mirror. By evening, they had searched all the seven cottages without any success. Xoxo had faded away. Thankfully, he could still talk and guide them.

'WE WILL GO HOME NOW. ALL OF YOU ARE TIRED. WE'LL BEGIN EARLY TOMORROW MORNING.'

They nodded glumly. They went out of the last abandoned house. Suddenly, Opal exclaimed loudly, 'Look, there is another house behind this cottage. It is exactly like our house. But how can this be possible? It is such a large house that we would have noticed it. But it looks exactly like our house.'

'YES, I WAS AFRAID OF THIS RIGHT FROM THE BEGINNING,' Xoxo said loudly, 'THE EVIL GHOSTS HAVE DUPLICATED YOUR HOUSE BUT ON THIS SIDE OF THE PADDY FIELDS. YOU HAVE TO BE ALERT ALL THE TIME. IF BY CHANCE YOU ENTERED THIS DUPLICATE HOUSE YOU WILL BE CAPTURED IN IT FOREVER, AND THERE WILL BE NO ESCAPE. WE DON'T KNOW WHAT AND WHERE THEY HAVE DUPLICATED. WE HAVE TO BE CAREFUL NOT TO BE FOOLED BY A COPIED IMAGE.'

Shailendra asked, 'Does this mean they can duplicate us human beings too?'

'I HAVE YET TO SEE THAT,' answered Xoxo, 'ONLY GOD HAS THE POWER TO CREATE LIFE AS IT SHOULD BE CREATED. IT COULD BE HUMAN BEINGS OR ANY OTHER FORM OF LIFE. IF THESE EVIL GHOSTS AND THE EVIL MIRROR DUPLICATE A HUMAN BEING, IT WON'T BE A REAL HUMAN. IT WILL LOOK LIKE A HUMAN BEING, BUT IT WILL BE LIKE A MACHINE CONTROLLED BY THESE CREATURES,' Xoxo said with distaste.

'Oh!' Shailendra excitedly announced, 'Let us continue with our search. We will not go home tonight but search for this mirror. Every minute is so dangerous.'

'No, Shailendra, we cannot do that,' Krish answered maturely, 'We are chasing ghosts with the help of a ghost who lives with us in our house. If we don't go home now, your parents will come searching for us at night, maybe with friends and the police too. That will put an end to our mission. We are hungry; Xoxo and Chutney are hungry, too. We will be asked so many questions that, sooner or later, we will tell them the truth. That will not do. We have to keep our mission as secret as possible.'

'Oh,' Shailendra said sheepishly, 'I hadn't thought of these reactions from our parents. Of course, they will come searching for us. Thanks, Krish bhaiya, let us go home now. We will come back early tomorrow.'

They went home. Once near their home, they began getting the smell of good comfort food coming from the kitchen.

'I wonder what mummy has made,' Opal mused.

All of them were suddenly very hungry. They rushed upstairs, cleaned themselves, ran down and began hogging the food. But not before Krish cleaned Chutney and fed him. Chutney, too, was tired. He went to sleep immediately afterwards. Xoxo was already there, sitting at the far end and inhaling the various aromas. Neelam had made *paneer koftas* and lentil-stuffed *parathas*. She had also made their favourite salad–iceberg lettuce, cucumber, onions, soaked almonds, walnuts, and raisins with a simple dressing of honey, lime juice, salt, and pepper. For dessert, they had fruit custard. After stuffing themselves, they went off straight to bed. They had to get up early tomorrow morning.

***

Into the Wild

The next day, they rushed through breakfast, packed their backpacks, and hurriedly went out. Opal ensured she had packed all of Xoxo's essential needs including the peacock feather fan. Shailendra helped her while Krish was double-checking his backpack for all the necessary items like a torch, matches, candles, knives, one for him and one for Shailendra, and many other things. Neelam was surprised to see them hurrying off, but she was not worried. Had she known what they were up to, she would have panicked and not allowed them out of the house.

Once they reached the thick part of the jungle, Opal took out the various essential oils and the peacock fan and passed them on to Xoxo. Xoxo was already nourished with the grand aromas of last night's dinner and today's breakfast. He now inhaled the tea tree oil deeply and began taking shape.

'HELLO, KRISH, OPAL AND CYLINDER. GOOD MORNING,' said Xoxo in a deep voice.

'Xoxo,' Shailendra protested, 'My name is not Cylinder, it is Shailendra.'

Xoxo tried to say Shailendra, but somehow, the words got so twisted in his tongue that Shailendra laughingly allowed him to call him Cylinder.

'But mind you, only till this mission. After that you have to practice and get my name right.'

Xoxo, who looked like a bedsheet hung on a pole, swung, and nodded in agreement.

They became serious. They had to find out the magic mirror today and destroy it.

'Look, there's our duplicate house again,' Shailendra exclaimed, 'But it seems to be fading at the edges. Why is this, Xoxo?'

'THIS IS A SORT OF A RELIEF TOO. IT MEANS THAT EITHER THE EVIL GHOSTS COULD NOT USE THE EVIL MIRROR PROPERLY, OR THE MAGIC OF THE EVIL MIRROR IS NOT STRONG ENOUGH TO DUPLICATE THINGS PERMANENTLY. EITHER WAY, IT IS WRONG TO DUPLICATE A THING HALFWAY AND LEAVE IT LIKE THAT. IMAGINE IF THEY WERE TO DUPLICATE A LIVING BEING AND LEAVE IT ONLY HALF-FORMED. IT WILL BE BAD BOTH FOR THE ORIGINAL AND THE DUPLICATE. BUT DON'T WORRY, WE'LL SOON FIND THE EVIL MAGIC MIRROR.'

Krish gave the instructions, 'Since we have already searched the abandoned houses, we will now, begin with the trees and the foliage near the stream and then the

Jungle Jalebi tree. Be very careful, don't pluck the fruits and don't even think of eating them! And everybody keep an eye on Chutney. Don't let him stray anywhere.'

'Don't worry, bhaiya,' Opal laughed, 'I have brought his new leash, though I'll put it on him only when things become serious.'

'Good girl,' Krish smiled at her, 'Now let's go to the stream.'

They marched towards the stream carefully as every bit of that part of the jungle was dangerous.

'ALL OF YOU GO AND SEARCH NEAR THE STREAM. I'LL GO TO THE OTHER SIDE OF THE JUNGLE. IF, BY CHANCE, I GET A GLIMPSE OF THE EVIL MIRROR, I WILL QUICKLY CALL ALL OF YOU. THE SAME GOES FOR YOU, GUYS. IF YOU FIND ANYTHING SUSPICIOUS, HOLLER AT THE TOP OF YOUR VOICE. I'LL FLY DOWN THERE IN A SECOND.'

They heard him and nodded abstractedly. They were too focused on their search. Xoxo floated away, and they went towards the stream. Chutney stopped and sniffed at every bit of foliage, and that slowed them down. Opal had to put him on his leash. Initially, Chutney did not like it and tried to shake out, but later, he happily adjusted when he found he was with them only.

They carefully walked near the stream, thoroughly searching the plants and trees. They peered in the moving water of the spring. They did not find anything which resembled or reflected anything. After two hours or so, they sat down to take a break. Shailendra opened their backpacks and took out their food. They then waited for Opal to give Chutney his milk. While eating their chicken sandwiches and apples, they saw Xoxo shimmering towards them.

'Any luck, Xoxo?' Krish asked him.

Xoxo gave a nod, then came and sat with them to have his lunch. Opal took out Xoxo's lunch, which consisted of a couple of chocolate biscuits, one open chicken sandwich for him to smell, his tea tree oil, and a bottle of paint. Xoxo took deep breaths of everything while the children ate their food. After finishing his lunch, Shailendra began brushing Xoxo with the peacock feather fan. They waited for Xoxo to get his breath and shape back. They were unsure whether Xoxo needed oxygen to be in this world.

After some time, Xoxo began, 'I AM NOT VERY SURE, BUT I THINK THE WICKED GHOSTS HAVE HIDDEN THE EVIL MAGIC MIRROR IN THE JUNGLE JALEBI TREE. YOU ALL KNOW THAT THEY HAVE DUPLICATED THE JUNGLE JALEBI TREE. I THINK THEY HAVE HIDDEN THE MIRROR IN THE REAL JUNGLE JALEBI TREE.'

'What makes you say that, Xoxo?' Krish asked him seriously.

'WELL, FOR ONE, WE ALL KNOW WHERE THE REAL JUNGLE JALEBI TREE IS. IT IS BESIDE THE STREAM NEAR YOUR HOUSE. THE FAKE JUNGLE JALEBI TREE IS ON THE OTHER SIDE OF THE PADDY FIELDS. IT IS LARGER THAN THE ORIGINAL TREE HERE. IT IS MUCH BRIGHTER, AND ITS FRUITS AND LEAVES TOO ARE MUCH LARGER IN NUMBER THAN THE REAL TREE. THE DUPLICATE TREE HAS MORE FOLIAGE, THAT IS, IT HAS MUCH MORE LEAVES AND MORE BRIGHTLY COLOURED FRUITS. HOW IS THIS POSSIBLE? I'VE THOUGHT ABOUT IT. I THINK THE EVIL GHOSTS ARE JUST PLAYING AROUND WITH THE MAGIC MIRROR AND

USING THE JUNGLE JALEBI TREE AND THE OTHER THINGS AROUND HERE, LIKE YOUR HOUSE, TO GET A HANG OF IT. IN OTHER WORDS, THEY ARE TRAINING THEMSELVES. ONCE THEY FULLY MASTER IT, THEY WILL DUPLICATE THE REAL EVIL THINGS WITH FULL CONFIDENCE. THAT IS WHY YOUR DUPLICATE HOME IS FADING AT THE EDGES AND, IN A MATTER OF DAYS, COULD FADE COMPLETELY. EVEN THE TREE, THEY ARE REPEATEDLY DUPLICATING ITS DIFFERENT PARTS AND FRUITS. THAT IS WHY SOME PARTS OF THE TREE ARE SO THICK, AND SOME ARE JUST NORMAL.'

That was quite a big speech for Xoxo's standards. His voice and he were intermittently dimming and glowing. Shailendra hurriedly gave him the tea tree oil to smell. Opal softly brushed him with the peacock feather fan. Xoxo took a few deep breaths. His voice and his body settled down a bit. He stopped. He was tired. Chutney went to him, gave him a few licks, and went to sleep on his feet.

'So now we have to figure out where the evil magic mirror could be. We can guess that the mirror is somewhere here, as the wicked ghosts are experimenting with it in this area,' Krish mused.

Xoxo kept quiet. He was still collecting his strength.

'I think they have hidden the mirror in the fake jungle jalebi tree,' Opal thought aloud, 'They use it at night so that nobody can see the tree or its fruits increasing in numbers.'

'Good guess, Oppie,' Shailendra praised her. Xoxo and Krish, too, nodded. Opal smiled happily.

'I think now we should go to the duplicate jungle jalebi tree and try to find the evil mirror,' Krish announced and looked at Xoxo. Xoxo had got his breath back by now. He, too, nodded.

'MIND YOU, DO IT CAREFULLY; DON'T PLUCK THE FRUITS AND UNDER NO CIRCUMSTANCE EAT OR RUB THEM.'

'We know. Xoxo,' Shailendra answered laughingly, 'You have become our guardian.'

They all smiled, except for Xoxo. He knew that, as a ghost, he should not have these protective feelings for the children. But he controlled himself. He would think about this later after they had destroyed the evil mirror.

So off they went to the duplicate jungle jalebi tree, searching for the mirror. After an hour or so, they could not find it despite rummaging thoroughly. They sat down near the tree, disappointed and tired. Even Xoxo was puzzled. He was sure the wicked ghosts had hidden the mirror in this tree.

'We will have to change our tactic now,' Krish declared, 'The tree is so lush with fruits and leaves that we are getting lost in them. Maybe if we cut down all the duplicated branches and fruits, we will be able to find the evil mirror.'

'THAT IS AN INTELLIGENT SOLUTION, KRISH,' Xoxo praised him, **'THEY CANNOT HIDE THE REAL EVIL MIRROR IN THE FAKE LEAVES AND FRUITS BECAUSE THEY ARE FAKE AND CAN VANISH ANYTIME. THE REAL LEAVES AND FRUITS WILL HIDE THE MIRROR FOR A LONG TIME. NOW, THE POINT IS TO DIFFERENTIATE BETWEEN THE DUPLICATE AND THE REAL ONES. I CAN THINK OF TWO OR THREE WAYS. THE FIRST ONE IS THAT THE DUPLICATED ONES ARE BRIGHTER AND MORE COLOURFUL THAN THE REAL ONES. YOU HAVE TO BE CAREFUL, BUT YOU CAN FIND THE DIFFERENCE. SECOND IS THAT YOU CAN GIVE CHUTNEY ONE LEAF**

OR ONE FRUIT. IF HE SEES OR LICKS IT, THEN IT IS THE REAL THING, AND WE SHOULD SEARCH THAT BRANCH. IF CHUTNEY DOESN'T SEE IT OR IGNORES IT, THEN THAT IS THE FAKE OR DUPLICATE BRANCH. I CAN ALSO FIND THE FAKE AND THE REAL LEAVES AND FRUITS, BUT THAT WILL TAKE TOO MUCH ENERGY; I MAY FADE OUT VERY SOON.'

The children readily agreed. They were now happy that Chutney would also play an active role in the operation. Between the three of them, they did have three knives, though of various sizes. Opal was not allowed knives, though she did have a small knife in her bag. Shailendra had a bigger one, and Krish had the best knife for their purpose. It was an army knife, serrated on one side and sharp on the other side. His parents had allowed him on the condition that he would not use it anywhere apart from using it on wood.

They would have to do with whatever they had.

'One question, Xoxo,' it was Shailendra, 'What happens after we find the evil magic mirror? Won't the evil ghosts try to save it? Won't they hurt us in the process? What should we do if they attack us?'

'OUR PRIORITY SHOULD BE TO PROTECT OURSELVES. ONLY THEN CAN WE PROTECT OTHERS. I KNOW WHAT THESE EVIL GHOSTS ARE AFRAID OF. THEY ARE EVIL BUT NOT VERY POWERFUL. THEY HAVE AN INSTRUMENT TO CREATE HAVOC, IF ONLY MOMENTARILY. THE EVIL MAGIC MIRROR CAN ONLY DUPLICATE THINGS FOR A SHORT TIME, FOR A COUPLE OF DAYS. ITS DUPLICATES ARE NOT PERMANENT. BUT STILL, THEY ARE ENOUGH TO CAUSE GREAT CONFUSION AND ENMITY IN A LARGE NUMBER OF PEOPLE. THESE THOUGHTS AND EVIL ACTIONS WILL NOT GO AWAY EVEN AFTER THE DUPLICATES VANISH. WHAT THESE EVIL

GHOSTS ARE MOST SCARED OF IS FIRE. FIRE IN ANY FORM—SMALL OR LARGE. EVEN I HAVE TO BE CAREFUL OF FIRE. SO WHAT YOU HAVE TO DO NOW FIRST IS TO COLLECT DRY LEAVES, DRY TWIGS, BRANCHES, AND OTHER DRY THINGS WHICH CAN BE BURNT IMMEDIATELY. I HOPE YOU HAVE A LIGHTER OR A MATCHBOX TO MAKE A FIRE?'

They nodded. Krish had both–a matchbox and a lighter, while Shailendra had a lighter. Opal was not allowed any of these things, but she was a happy and adaptable girl. She suggested, 'I'll gather dry leaves, twigs and other dry things so that we are ready if and when the Evils attack us.'

'That's a good idea, Oppie,' Shailendra patted her shoulder, 'Make small heaps all around the jungle jalebi tree so that they don't escape with or without the magic mirror.'

'Yes, bhaiya, I'll do that; come Chutney, you can help me,' Chutney wagged his tail as if he understood everything and ran ahead of Opal. Krish and Shailendra went towards the jungle jalebi tree and stared at it. They were trying to differentiate the real tree from its duplicated parts. Xoxo was with them.

'WE WILL BEGIN FROM THE FAR END OF THE TREE, WHERE THERE IS MORE FOLIAGE. THESE EVILS HAVE NO IDEA OF SYMMETRY. THEY HAVE INCREASED THE FOLIAGE MUCH MORE IN THE BACK AND NOT MUCH IN THE FRONT. WE WILL FIRST HACK THE FAKE FOLIAGE AT THE BACK.'

The boys nodded. There wasn't much time. If they left their work midway and continued the next day, the Evils would shift and take the evil mirror somewhere else. Nobody would know where they went. Xoxo could know, but for that, he would have to follow them. Xoxo was not the usual kind of a powerful, wicked ghost. He was a good ghost but physically weak, one who got his strength from the smell of good food and a few other things. The children had kept his supply of aromatic food always ready. He would harm only himself if he chased the evil ghosts. Hence, it was important that they find the evil mirror today itself. And before it got dark. They were naturally not allowed to stay in the jungle after dark.

They quickly went to the other side of the jungle jalebi tree, which was full of heavy leaves and fruits. It was so bright, tempting and attractive, and they were children. But the thought of eating the bright red and pink fruits did not enter their minds. They focused on their task of finding the evil magic mirror. And they had to do it fast. They began cutting down the fake branches, leaves, and fruits. Another magic awaited them. As these duplicated branches fell on the ground, they fizzled out and ultimately vanished. That was good for the boys as they didn't want to cut any genuine part of the tree.

Suddenly, there was a loud thud which came from the tree. They stopped, unsure of what to do. Shailendra looked around for Opal. She had collected quite a big pile of dried leaves and other debris from the jungle. Now, she was making small mounds of these things, placing them around the tree. Chutney was yipping and barking merrily and following Opal. Once in a while, he would dive inside the mound of leaves and shrubbery and shake everything loose.

'Chutney! Now you've spoilt this mound! I'll have to make it again. Don't do it again, okay? Otherwise, I'll have to put the leash on you.'

Chutney barked and gave his assent. But Opal became more careful. She didn't want to put the leash on him.

The loud sound seemed as if something huge had fallen from the tree. It could be a branch or anything. It could be a ghost, too. But as far as their experience and knowledge went, ghosts were as weightless as the wind. But something heavy did fall and scramble to get up. Shailendra rushed towards Opal and Chutney while Krish turned his knife towards the sound. Though Krish couldn't see anything, he could hear the sounds of scuffling as if two persons were fighting or helping each other to get up. He turned towards Xoxo. Xoxo, too, was shifting into his vanishing mode. But he was responsible enough to reassure Krish.

'DON'T BE NERVOUS KRISH. THESE TWO ARE JUST TWO STUPID, LAZY GHOSTS WHOSE SLEEP MUST HAVE BEEN DISTURBED. THEY FELL AS THE BRANCHES OF THE TREE SHOOK. THEY ARE LIKE SCARED KITTENS. THEY HAUNT PEOPLE AND SOMETIMES THEMSELVES FOR THE SILLIEST REASONS. THAT IS WHY THEIR POSSESSING THE MAGIC DUPLICATING MIRROR IS ALL THE MORE DANGEROUS. THEY'LL DUPLICATE ANYTHING JUST BECAUSE THEY FEEL LIKE IT OR WANT TO HAVE SOME FUN. THEY GET SCARED VERY EASILY, AND THEIR ONLY THOUGHT NOW IS TO ESCAPE AND CLIMB ANOTHER TREE TO GO BACK TO SLEEP. THE EVIL GHOSTS MAY OR MAY NOT BE THERE. WE WILL FACE THEM IF THEY COME IN FRONT OF US. OUR AIM SHOULD BE ONLY TO FIND AND DESTROY THE MAGIC MIRROR.'

Krish nodded. He, too, wanted the whole thing to be over now. He went on hacking those branches that were either too bright or looked fake. Xoxo had almost disappeared. Krish called out to Shailendra, 'Shailendra, bring the biscuits and the other oils which Xoxo likes to smell. His power has almost gone.'

'Yes, Krish bhaiya, I was coming with them anyway. Now is the time for Xoxo to be fully with us. We should hear and see him properly,' then, turning to Opal he said, 'Oppie, just give a loud shout if you feel any danger.'

'Yes, bhaiya,' Opal was busy with her work. She had almost completed one round of putting heaped mounds of dry leaves and twigs around the jungle jalebi tree, 'There is more than enough dried jungle debris here, bhaiya. I'll make a second ring of them around the tree so there is no chance of the Evils escaping with the evil magic mirror.'

'You do that, Oppie; I'll go and revive Xoxo and then help Krish bhaiya with hacking the duplicate parts of the tree.'

Shailendra put the chocolate vanilla biscuits and a few strong-smelling salts and oils on a plate and went and stood in front of Xoxo. Xoxo would not hold the plate as that would also require energy. He had to conserve all his energy in guiding the children and ensuring they did not get into danger. He deeply inhaled the lovely smells of the biscuits, the tea tree oil, and the other oils which Opal and Shailendra had kept for him. Shailendra kept on patting him with the peacock fan, too.

After some time, when he got his voice and form back, he spoke to Shailendra, **'KEEP THE PLATE NEAR ME**

CYLINDER, I CAN LOOK AFTER MYSELF NOW. YOU GO TO THE MIDDLE OF THIS JUNGLE JALEBI TREE AND START HACKING THE BRANCHES THERE. ALL THE BRANCHES THERE ARE DUPLICATES.'

Shailendra nodded and went towards the middle part of the tree. He also knew there wasn't much time left and their weapons were not up to the mark. After all, they only carried small knives and matches and a lighter.

After an hour or so, they had completely removed all the duplicates. Now, only the natural branches and fruits were left. They now earnestly began searching for the evil magic mirror. They shook the leaves, the branches, and the fruits, with Xoxo directing them to the places where he thought the mirror would be.

'Krish bhaiya, I cannot shake this branch. It's solid like an iron pole, and the leaves are not shaking either.'

Xoxo was just behind them, **'WAIT!'** he shrieked, **'DON'T LET GO OF THAT BRANCH. JUST HOLD ONTO IT.'**

Shailendra froze. Was he holding the handle of the mirror?

***

Mission Possible?

As if in slow motion, he saw and heard Krish running towards him. Krish rushed towards Shailendra, and he too tightly gripped the branch that Shailendra was holding. Together, the two of them pulled at it. But it didn't move even a millimetre. They looked at Xoxo, who was flapping his wing-like tent and seemed flustered.

'**DON'T LET GO OF IT! IT IS THE EVIL MAGIC MIRROR. DON'T LOOK AT IT STRAIGHT. IT MAY DUPLICATE PARTS OF YOU, WHICHEVER PARTS IT SEES. CUT A FEW BRANCHES THAT WILL LOOSEN IT,**' Xoxo directed them.

Shailendra held on to the branch while Krish began hacking the smaller branches and leaves attached to it. After some time, the main branch began loosening up a bit. Now, it started looking like a handle. Both the brothers now began pulling at it with all their strength. But before they could loosen it, there was a big sound of things falling from the tree. Distracted, they stopped.

'CYLINDER,' said Xoxo urgently, 'GO TO OPAL IMMEDIATELY, TELL HER TO PICK UP CHUTNEY AND RUN FAR AWAY FROM THIS TREE. THEN, BURN ALL THE DRIED RUBBLE THAT OPAL HAS COLLECTED AROUND THE TREE. THE SOUND THAT YOU HEARD IS THE SOUND OF THE EVIL GHOSTS FALLING FROM THE TREE. THEY ARE NOT TOO POWERFUL AND A BIT SCARED NOW. THEY HAVE SEEN YOUR KNIVES. THEY WILL WANT TO ESCAPE WITH THE EVIL MIRROR NOW. BUT YOUR STRENGTH IS MORE THAN THEIRS. KRISH, DON'T LET GO OF THE MIRROR UNDER ANY CIRCUMSTANCES. PULL IT OUT OF THE SHRUB WITH YOUR FULL STRENGTH. ALONG WITH THAT, SLASH YOUR KNIFE IN THE AIR IN ALL DIRECTIONS. THAT WILL SCARE THEM, AND THEY WILL RUN AWAY. THE FIRE WILL BE BURNING AROUND THE TREE. SO THEY WILL AGAIN COME TO THE TREE. AS SOON AS THEY RUN, YOU, TOO, RUN OUT WITH THE MIRROR. BUT WHILE THE EVIL GHOSTS WILL COME BACK, YOU JUMP OVER THE FIRE AND ESCAPE WITH THE MIRROR. GO BACK NEAR YOUR HOME WITH OPAL AND CYLINDER, AND I WILL FOLLOW YOU AFTER A FEW MINUTES.'

Krish and Shailendra nodded. Shailendra ran towards where Opal was still collecting the twigs and dry leaves. He took out the Krish's lighter and began lighting the mounds of the dry shrubs that Opal had collected. He then picked up Chutney in his lap and took Opal's hand. Opal was alarmed, 'Bhaiya, what are you doing? We can't run away, leaving Krish bhaiya and Xoxo there. The mirror is still there!'

Shailendra panted, 'There is no time for explanations, Oppie. Xoxo has told us to run as fast as we can. I will explain later.'

Opal was puzzled, but she could sense the emergency. She held tightly to Shailendra's hand, and they ran towards their home.

Though Opal ran fast with Shailendra, she kept looking back too, for Krish bhaiya and Xoxo.

In the meantime, in the huge jungle jalebi tree, the evil ghosts tried to pull the magic mirror away from Krish. But Krish did not lose his confidence. He firmly held the mirror's handle in his left hand and brandished the knife with his left hand.

As Xoxo had claimed, these evil ghosts did not have the physical strength of Krish, a strong boy. These ghosts were just like wisps of thick air. At one time, Krish's knife connected with the middle of one of the ghosts. His body was almost severed in half, and he fell. But he quickly recovered, and soon, the two parts of his body joined together. Physically, they were no match to Krish, who kept waving his knife all around him. He must have slashed them some more times; he did not know as he could not see them. He could just feel them.

'That's all, Krish, they have finally run away. Now, when they reach the fire around the tree, they will rush back. Fire has the power to destroy them permanently. You will have to be very careful and quick about it. There will hardly be any time. In their panic they will run faster than usual. You have to be faster than them. Keep the magic mirror with yourself, rush and jump over the fire and run towards your home. Don't go inside your home; wait for me because even I have to avoid the fire.'

Krish nodded, placed the magic mirror and knife

inside his jacket, zipped it up and then ran towards the circle of fire surrounding the tree. He was so charged up with the whole adventure that he jumped high over the fire without any hesitation and cleared it easily. He fell on the grass on the other side of the fire and gasped for breath. In a jiffy, he was on his feet again. He began running towards their home with his hands over his jacket where he had put the mirror. Very soon, he arrived where Opal and Shailendra were waiting for him. Chutney wagged his tail crazily on seeing him, climbed on his lap and licked his face all over. Krish hugged him laughingly.

'Are you alright, bhaiya?' Shailendra asked him, 'Do you have the mirror? Where is Xoxo?'

'He'll be coming in a few minutes. He is also scared of the fire. When the fire dies down, the Evils will go up in the jungle jalebi tree and hide there. Xoxo will jump over the fire and come to us. Opal, keep his food and smells and the peacock fan ready. He will be very exhausted; we may not be able to see him and talk to him for some time.'

They sat and waited for Xoxo. They did not know when he finally came. It was Chutney who jumped out of Krish's lap and went and began wagging his tail and licking the air.

'Xoxo! You've finally come!' Opal exclaimed happily, 'Here, get some strength first,' she took two plates to him–one had the delicious-smelling biscuits and two pieces of cakes, and the other plate had small bottles of tea tree oil and other liquids with strong, pungent aromas. They then waited for Xoxo to catch his breath and gather his strength. They were quite exhausted, though they did not feel their exhaustion because of their excitement. The only person who was not really concerned by the happenings was Chutney. His loved ones were there, he had just been fed by Opal–he did not need anything else.

Xoxo recovered after fifteen minutes or so. They could now see him, though he was still hazy.

'ALL OF YOU ARE ADMIRABLE CHILDREN. EVEN ADULTS WOULD NOT HAVE BEEN ABLE TO DO WHAT YOU HAVE ACCOMPLISHED TODAY. BUT THERE IS STILL THE MOST IMPORTANT WORK LEFT,' he paused and took a deep breath.

'We have to get rid of the mirror,' Krish announced, 'How should we do it? Should we break it into pieces and then bury it? Will the Evils be able to put it back together? Should we use some other method?' Krish mused.

'NOW LISTEN TO ME VERY CAREFULLY. I MAY NOT HAVE THE PROPER STRENGTH TO REPEAT THE INSTRUCTIONS. THERE ARE TWO, RATHER THREE WAYS WHICH WE HAVE TO COMBINE TO DESTROY THE EVIL MIRROR. FIRST, YOU WILL HAVE TO BREAK IT WITH YOUR KNIFE, KRISH. AFTER IT BREAKS INTO SMALL PIECES, YOU WILL HAVE TO BURN IT. AND THEN, FINALLY, YOU HAVE TO BURY IT DEEP INSIDE THE GROUND. FOR MORE SAFETY, WE WILL KEEP YOUR LIGHTER BESIDE THE CRUSHED MIRROR. IF THE EVILS FIND IT, THEY WILL BE SCARED TO TOUCH IT BECAUSE OF THE FIRE THAT MAY FLARE OUT FROM THE LIGHTER.'

'But Xoxo, why break it with the knife? Why not with a hammer or a stone?' asked Shailendra.

'FROM ANCIENT TIMES, CYLINDER, THE ONLY WAY AN EVIL GHOST CAN BE DESTROYED IS BY KILLING IT WITH AN IRON KNIFE OR BURNING IT. I DON'T KNOW THE HISTORY BEHIND IT, BUT THAT IS THE WAY IT is done. You can do some research on it after we complete this work. Now, be very careful when you are crushing the mirror. Keep it covered by a cloth or paper as even its smaller pieces may have the power to duplicate things and maybe living things too. We do not want a duplicate arm or leg or even half a dog,' Xoxo declared.

They all nodded. Xoxo's last sentence had really sobered them up. Nobody wanted their body parts duplicated. Opal took a towel from her bag and gave it to Krish and Shailendra, who carefully covered the mirror. Opal held Chutney tightly, just in case he jumped on the mirror with excitement. But Chutney was tired after the day's happenings. Opal had fed him, too. He just curled in her lap and went to sleep.

Krish took out his knife. It wasn't a strong or very sharp knife. He struck the evil magic mirror with the knife with all his strength. Nothing happened; the mirror just slipped a bit away from the knife. They all knew the knife was not strong enough to easily break the mirror, but it had an iron blade. So, both Krish and Shailendra took turns to hit it. Krish was afraid the blade might break if they hit it too hard. Krish turned to Xoxo, 'Xoxo, my knife might break, the mirror is too hard. Can we break it first with a stone and then use the knife on the smaller pieces?'

Even Xoxo was watching their efforts with complete interest. He was thinking. What Krish said made sense, though he was unsure of the outcome. It was going to be dark in some time. They had to go home. The evil mirror could not be left here, nor could it be taken home. Reluctantly, he agreed, though he was still in two minds. But there was no other choice.

Shailendra ran and collected three large, heavy rocks, and then he and Krish started bashing the mirror. This was much better. After some time, they heard the mirror cracking and knew it had broken into several pieces. They could not see it in the hand towel. Krish then took the knife and plunged it into the wrapped mirror. This time, the mirror broke. Krish kept plunging the knife into the wrapped mirror to stab every piece with the knife. He stopped only when he was sure that all the pieces of the mirror had been broken by the knife.

'**GOOD WORK, KRISH,**' Xoxo approved. They could hear the relief in his voice. '**WE NOW HAVE TO BURY THESE BROKEN PIECES IN THE GROUND. CYLINDER, YOU CAN KEEP KRISH'S LIGHTER ON THE MIRROR SO THAT THE EVILS CAN FEEL THE PRESENCE OF FIRE AND NOT TRY TO DO ANY TRICKS.**'

Shailendra placed the lighter atop the hand towel wrapped around the mirror.

'Krish bhaiya, you look after the mirror while I dig a hole in the earth.'

Krish nodded. Shailendra began digging a hole in the ground nearby. Very soon, he had dug a neat, round and deep hole. Then he and Krish put the broken mirror inside the hole, covered it again with mud and stamped on it to ensure the package was firmly entrenched inside.

They sat down on the ground to catch their breaths. They were quiet for some time, each wrapped in their own thoughts. Soon, Opal spoke, 'Tell me, Xoxo, what will those evil ghosts do now? Their entertainment is gone and completely destroyed now. Will they continue being cruel to animals and the jungle now?'

There was silence from the place where Xoxo was sitting. Was he there, or had he gone somewhere? But they heard something. It was Xoxo's raspy voice, **'OH, THEM! THEY ARE VAGABONDS AND ARE TOO SCARED TO DO ANYTHING NOW. THEY ARE THE KIND WHO TAKE PLEASURE IN JUST SCARING PEOPLE. IT'S TRUE THAT THEY DON'T HAVE A KIND HEART, BUT THEY GET FRIGHTENED VERY EASILY. THEY GOT THE SCARE OF THEIR LIVES OR DEATHS TODAY. I KNOW THEY HAVE RUN AWAY FROM THIS PLACE EVEN AS WE SPEAK. THEY WILL RUN AWAY TO ANOTHER JUNGLE, THIS TIME TO A DENSE JUNGLE WHERE NO ONE GOES. THERE, THEY WILL EAT SOME SMALL ANIMALS AND GO FOR A LONG SLEEP.'**

Shailendra was looking thoughtfully at Xoxo, 'What about you, Xoxo? What will you do now?'

There was silence again on Xoxo's side, and then, he spoke, **'WHAT ABOUT ME? NOTHING. I'VE GOT A LOVING FAMILY AFTER SUCH A LONG TIME. I WOULD LIKE TO STAY IN MY OWN HOUSE, THAT IS, IF ALL OF YOU ALLOW ME,'** Xoxo asked.

Opal went and sat beside Xoxo, 'Oh Xoxo, how can you even think of going anywhere else? Our home is your home first. In fact we are the trespassers. Xoxo, will you allow us to stay in your home, at least till the time…' she stopped herself.

The others looked at her, puzzled. What did she mean? But Xoxo understood, **'YOU ARE MOST WELCOME, ALL OF YOU. WHERE WILL I GET SUCH MAGICAL AROMAS OF DELICIOUS FOOD!'** they laughed. Xoxo got serious, **'WHEN I WAS ALIVE, I**

HAD MADE A WILL AND NOW I JUST CAN'T REMEMBER WHERE I HAD HIDDEN IT. I WILL NOT LOOK FOR IT AT ALL NOW. ALL OF YOU CAN STAY IN MY HOUSE FOR AS LONG AS YOU WANT. I, TOO, WANT TO STAY WITH YOU AS LONG AS I CAN, AND GO FOR MANY MORE ADVENTURES IF THAT IS ALRIGHT?' he asked. His shadowy figure showed itself for a minute. They hugged him, and Chutney licked him, **'I WILL HAVE TO GO WHEN HE CALLS ME,'** Xoxo looked up.

'Xoxo, we want you to stay with us forever,' Opal declared. Xoxo gave a watery smile. They couldn't see him, but they knew that he was smiling.

'OKAY, AFTER A FEW DAYS WHEN WE GET OUR STRENGTH BACK WE HAVE ANOTHER ADVENTURE WAITING FOR US.'

The others looked at him with curiosity.

'WE HAVE TO SEARCH FOR MY MAGIC COMPASS. IT TELLS US ABOUT THE PRESENCE OF GHOSTS AMONG MANY OTHER THINGS...' His voice faded away. They knew that he had run out of energy. Opal gave him some sniffs of tea tree oil so he could at least walk home. After that, their mother's cooking and its aromas would take care of him.

It was late evening now. They packed up their things and started back towards their home. They were quiet on the way back. The whole adventure was slowly sinking into them now. They had performed a huge feat almost effortlessly. But it would take days and even weeks for them to stop thinking about what they had done and how they had managed to avert a great catastrophe. Chutney was now being carried by Shailendra. Krish was too overwhelmed by what they had just done.

Opal was too tired to hold Chutney. They knew that Xoxo was with them, though they could not see or hear him. They could feel his presence. Somehow, they reached home. Neelam saw them and was surprised, 'Well, well, today I think you all went on a really big adventure. All of you are looking so dirty and scruffy. Hurry up with your baths and come for dinner.'

'What is there for dinner, Chachi?' Krish was getting some of his breath back.

'Everybody's favourite *beta, biryani* and *kebabs* with *raita*,' they perked up a bit and went upstairs. Neelam was a bit puzzled. They did not show much enthusiasm. 'Maybe they are really exhausted. The dinner will perk them up. Why am I getting a feeling that they are already enjoying the food?' She shrugged her shoulders. Little did she know that Xoxo was already there and was thoroughly inhaling and enjoying the smells of the delicious food. This was combined with the success of their dangerous and anxious day. It was good that the peacock fan was not there, otherwise he may have taken form and then there would have been utter chaos.

The children came down, looking very clean, but tired too. They ate their food with enthusiasm but were subdued. Their adventure and victory had started sinking in. But they were too tired to even talk about it. They had their food and immediately went to their rooms to sleep.

For tomorrow was another day.

***

Acknowledgements

Many people have been directly or indirectly involved in the publication of this book, which makes it difficult for me to single them out. My publisher, Renu Kaul Verma, has been instrumental in ensuring that my manuscripts become books. Without her continual support and vision, my books would not have seen the light of day. My editors, Vichitra Goel and Saumya Chaudhary are excellent at their job, giving pertinent and valuable suggestions. Somesh Kumar Mishra plays around with colours to bring my books to life. Saraswathi, Faiza, Prateek and the entire team of Vitasta have been a constant support. My humble thanks to each one of you for helping me throughout.

My sons, Saurabh and Sarvesh, along with their wives Shubhra and Deepika gave me immense moral support.

My grandchildren, Aaroh, Myra and Avitraya, knew what their dadi was committed to and often surprised me with their creative ideas. My husband and best friend, Arun, supported me every step of the way and without whose encouragement it would have been difficult to write these books.

About the Author

Shubira is an avid follower of the Indian epics. She has always found a new and unique interpretation with her every reading of epics like the Ramayana and Mahabharata. She believes we all have some demonic qualities that need to be overcome to bring out the best in us. She feels mythological stories are real happenings occurred so long ago that we failed to substantiate them.

Despite her deep understanding of the epics, Shubira never wanted to restrict herself to writing only mythological fantasies. After her Humans versus Demons trilogy, she wrote a romance and has now written a children's book in which three children and their pup have a rollicking adventure where they help a ghost save the world.

Shubira began her career as an educationist and has worked in educational institutions across the country. Having a keen interest in the human psyche, she did her Honours in Psychology and then her masters in English literature. Along with being a teacher, she is an astrologer too and has been writing articles on astrology and social issues. She is married to an Air Force officer and now lives in the National Capital Region.

SCAN ME

Other Books By The Author